RUNNER IN THE SUN

W9-BCN-501

RUNNER IN THE SUN

A Story of Indian Maize

by D'Arcy McNickle

Illustrated by Allan C. Houser
Afterword by Alfonso Ortiz

A Zia Book

UNIVERSITY OF NEW MEXICO PRESS
Albuquerque

To Roma, Tony, and Kay

Library of Congress Cataloging-in-Publication Data

McNickle, D'Arcy, 1904–1977.
    Runner in the sun.

(A Zia book)
    Summary: A story of pre-Hispanic Indian life in the
area which is now the American Southwest.
    1. Indians of North America—Southwest, New—
Juvenile fiction. [1. Indians of North America—
Southwest, New—Fiction] I. Houser, Allan C., ill.
II. Title. III. Series.
PZ7.M237Ru   1987   [Fic]   87-5986
ISBN 0-8263-0974-7

CONTENTS

Author's Foreword

MOST of us grow up believing that the history of America begins with the men who came across from Europe and settled in New World wilderness. The real story of our country is much older, much richer, than this usual history book account.

Thousands of years before Europeans, by accident, stumbled upon the American continents, men were living here, scattered between the two polar oceans. They lived under a variety of conditions, and they developed tools, clothing, shelter, food habits, customs, and beliefs to fit their conditions. In some areas, they felled trees in the forest and built houses out of planks split from the trees. Elsewhere, they erected great mounds of earth and stone and placed their houses and temples on the summits. In still other places, they quarried rock and built houses of stone.

They were skilled craftsmen and artists: weaving baskets; fashioning fine pottery; carving in wood, stone, and ivory; molding copper, silver, and gold ornaments; and rearing monumental public buildings. Some were fishermen and sea-mammal hunters, following their game in wooden boats far out in the open ocean. Others were renowned hunters of land animals. But by far the greater part of this population depended upon agriculture, and some groups even constructed irrigation works to reclaim otherwise worthless desert lands.

Salt's people lived without written records, but the shape and content of their lives have been pieced together by scientists examining the houses, tools, weapons, clothing, ceremonial objects, and other evidences of their existence. We know approximately when they lived, and what happened to them.

They were real people, as were all the people Salt encountered on his journey south into the country we call Mexico. They lived, looking into the very skies we look into, hundreds of years before Columbus and his three little ships set sail from Isabella's Spain.

They and their racial kinsmen, scattered over the two continents, domesticated many of the food, fiber, and medicinal plants we use today; not alone the corn which plays a part in our story, but tobacco, white and sweet potatoes, long staple cotton, beans, pumpkins, squash, cocoa, quinine, tomatoes, maguey fiber (henequen), and cassava (tapioca), to mention the best known. The tribes inhabiting the highlands of Peru used no fewer than seventy different plants for food and other purposes.

The world was enriched by such a material contribution as maize, or Indian corn, which quickly spread to all continents after New World discovery. The world might have been even richer today if the first Europeans had adopted and carried away with them the respect for peaceful living which characterized the first Americans.

Columbus remarked their gentle quality: "No request of anything from them is ever refused, but they rather invite acceptance of what they possess, and manifest such a generosity that they would give away their own hearts."

Later Europeans, coming as permanent settlers, would learn to dread the war cry of the wilderness, and they would depict the Indian as a dull, revengeful savage. Unfortunately for the Indian people, this latter judgment has prevailed.

The gentle, friendly people Columbus encountered did not physically disappear, but something happened to that openhanded generosity with which they met him. Tribes dislodged from their homes along the Atlantic coast had either to fight or perish. They turned upon other tribes, seeking territory, and soon Indian fought against Indian throughout the land. With mounting ferocity, they attacked white settlements as well, and border warfare did not finally subside until an awful morning in December 1890, when a camp of Sioux Indians was slaughtered in the snow on Wounded Knee Creek, South Dakota, by United States soldiers.

Scientists digging into old village sites tell us of tribes living side by side for hundreds of years without warfare. The myths and legends of the many tribes are not battle stories, but convey instead a feeling for the dignity of man and reverence for all of nature. Best of all evidence of the innate peace-seeking habits of the first Americans are the living Indian societies of today. Here one finds true concern for the well-being of each least member, respect for the elders, and devotion to the needs of the spirit.

Corn was, indeed, a great gift to the world; but a greater gift was one that the world let lie and never gathered up for its own. That was the gift of peace on earth.

Yes, these were real people. They broke the trails which our railways and highways follow today. Their names are upon our land, upon the rivers, lakes, and mountains we love.

They belong in the great tradition we call American.

Chapter 1

Call to the Kiva

THIS is the story of a town that refused to die. It is the story of the angry men who tried to destroy, and of the Indian boy called Salt, in the language of his people, who stood against them.

It was not an ordinary town. It did not rise from the crown of a hill and flash views of its towers and steeples to an approaching stranger. Neither did it fit snugly in a valley against the bend of a sparkling river. One might travel close by and never know the town existed, unless one had been told about it.

1

The country which held this town was so broad and flat that the horizon seemed to lie at the end of the world. The soil underfoot was light gray in color, but so thickly was the land covered with pinon and juniper and dwarf oak that the distances looked black. It was high country, a land of little rain, where rocks turned black under the sun's intensity. At day's end, after heat had poured for long hours upon the parched earth, waves of blue haze rose against the horizon until earth and sky blurred and the tops of distant turreted rocks seemed to float on empty space. The people living there sometimes called it the Enchanted Land.

If one traveled across the countryside looking for the town, one would come without warning to the edge of space. The broad plain with its grass and sage and pinion trees ceased to be. Looking down into the void one would see shadows, and at first it might seem that there was no bottom. The sun striking from an angle made a shimmering screen that blocked vision. After one's eyes became adjusted to the tricky light, a rock wall would float into view, ghostlike, across a wide chasm. By shielding one's eyes, details would come into focus. A jutting pinnacle of rock rose from the bottom. Pine and spruce trees appeared far below. A shaft of light might strike the bronze of an eagle's wings as it pivoted on a current of rising air.

At last the town would emerge out of shadow. It was not at the bottom of the chasm, but in the wall of gray rock standing opposite. Streaks of brown weathering extended downward from the top of the canyon, then disappeared where the rock bulged inward to form the roof of a cave. The houses inside the cave were perfectly sheltered. They were built of stone and stood in some places four stories high.

No smoke would rise from cooking fires; no life would be visible. Sun and shadow alone would be there. But listening carefully, it might seem, after a while, that sounds were rising from the canyon depths. Voices would be chanting faintly. The dead air would stir between the rock walls. The lazily vaulting eagle would clap its wings in startled energy and sail away.

This was the town where the boy called Salt lived many centuries ago. The path to the town—White Rock Place or Village, they called it—started from the bottom of a canyon. There was also a way to reach it from on top, where the people had their planted fields. In addition, a certain few old men knew of a secret trail, but this knowledge they guarded carefully, lest enemies learn of it and steal in upon the people while they slept.

The canyon floor was a clutter of great boulders fallen from the cliff during the centuries, when frost and wind and rain were gouging out the cave. Rocks had also decayed into earth and the earth produced a thick growth of succulent grasses and shrubs. The bottom of the canyon was cool and moist. A stream of clear water, starting from a gushing spring at the head of the canyon, twisted over and around the crowding boulders. The water flowed not so strongly as it once had; it made a feeble music among the boulders, but still it left the air smelling of sweet dampness. Willows, wild cherry, cottonwood, cedar, and tall yellow pines followed the stream bed, while hardier sage and juniper scrambled up the slope of the canyon until solid rock was encountered. Juniper is not easily discouraged, and single bushes clung to the rock wall, wherever a crack had allowed a seed to lodge. The canyon bottom was a pleasant place, where meadow larks sang even in the heat of midday and mourning doves talked to each other in pine tree shade.

The trail climbed an easy slope of fractured rock lying at the base of the cliff. Where the slope ended at the cliff wall, the trail followed a shelf of rock, then disappeared into a narrow cleft or chimney. It ascended by a succession of natural and carved steps until it reached another horizontal shelf. The last steep pitch was bridged by three thick logs, placed one above the other against rock buttresses. In time, children learned to run up and down these notched logs as if they were following a path on level ground. In case of attack the logs could be tossed down and the cave was then inaccessible from below.

The boy called Salt climbed the last log and stood finally within the cave, where he paused for breath. A burning early summer sun struck back from the gray walls across the canyon and even the deep interior of the cave was unusually bright. The boy liked the brightness and the burning feeling on his skin. He wanted not to move from the hot boulder against which he leaned.

This was the high end of the cave, and standing with his back to the wall he could see down into the village. People he talked to every day were moving about. A woman who often visited his mother was climbing the ladder that led into her house. No doors or windows occurred at the ground level and entrances were from the roof. An old blind man sat in the full sun spinning cotton into thread by rolling the loose fiber across his bare thigh. A second old man sat nearby and talked, no doubt about what everybody was talking about these days—the diminishing flow of the spring at the bottom of the canyon. Children and their dogs made faint shouting noises at the far end of the village. Salt watched them, then watched a man appear on the roof of the Chief's House. The man's voice came clearly, though faintly, up to Salt.

"Now hear your father speak!" Salt heard. The shell ornament at the man's throat flashed a miniature sun.

This was the Crier, and Salt knew without hearing the words what he would announce, and he knew without going further what the village fathers might talk about when in response to the announcement they assembled in the kiva of the Turquoise people.

A boy of sixteen already knew many things. Climbing about, and poking about, as a boy must if he is to learn things, Salt had seen men meeting when they thought they went unobserved. He had heard words exchanged in the darkness of night. He had come upon these things unexpectedly, then had crept closer, practicing his stealth. Then he realized that he was not playing a boy's game, and he became afraid.

Salt was slender, with a man's height. He was a straight line from shoulder to hip, and his long muscled legs suggested a tireless runner. His clothing was simple: a band of cloth wrapped around his shoulder-length black hair, and a kind of kilt held at his waist by a belt. The kilt was woven of white cotton with black zigzags running up and down. His feet were covered with sandals made of twisted yucca fiber which curved up and over his toes and were fastened by thongs crossing over the instep. Around his neck he wore white shells strung on a buckskin thong with a central ornament of turquoise inlaid in bone. But this was more than ornament—it signified his initiation into manhood. His frequent touching of it disclosed how new a thing it was for him to wear.

His face, as he watched in repose, had a gentle look. The eyes were large and set wide; the nose high and straight; the lips thin—a countenance promising intelligence and quick feeling. He tried to close his ears to the words rising from below, to pretend he did not hear and did not have to respond.

"Now hear, O children! The world once before died in fire and our fathers ran into the unwatered desert and slaked their thirst on burning sand. Do not bring the fires again to ravage us from our homes and drive livid snakes upon us! Heed this! Turquoise men, you are called by your fathers. Come at once to the underground house. Turquoise men, come to the clan house!"

Salt frowned. The words, born of a long-ago fear, were intended to bend the mind and compel instant obedience.

He recognized that the summons was for him. He was of the Turquoise people, and he must go. But he would go warily. If those men, those secret meeting men, charged him with spying, he would not be frightened. But really he would rather not go to the meeting!

The boy walked along the path which ran just inside a low masonry wall at the cliff's edge. He could peer easily over the wall into the depths of the canyon where, far below, pine and cedar made a deeper gloom. It was a view he gazed upon so many times a day that now he did not even see it.

Within the cave no space went unused. The buildings followed the contours of the cave floor and, where it sloped sharply, a house might be two stories in front and a single story in back. At the highest arch of the cave, buildings of three and four stories reached to the roof. One principal street, besides the path at the cliff's edge, ran the length of the village. It was a crooked street, narrow and wide by turns, as it crossed the village. A single opening led inward from the cliff path, but a stranger might never find the opening because it seemed to end against a blank wall. A sharp turn to the left, a narrow passage, then a flight of steps, led at last to an open space where public gatherings were held and where outdoor cooking fireplaces filled the air with the odor of sweet-smelling cedar.

Salt turned from the cliff path and at the stone steps found his way blocked by several small, naked children, watched over by two older girls wearing skirts, with woven bands to hold back their hair. The girls looked up, saw that the passage was blocked, but giggled and made no attempt to get their young charges out of the way. Salt felt affronted by their failure to recognize the urgency of his mission.

"I am called to the House of the Turquoise people. The men are gathering," he explained. The girls eyed him, but only giggled the harder.

A boy of four, round and brown, looked and grinned. Next moment, he came charging at Salt's legs and almost bowled him over. Salt saved himself by reaching down and lifting the urchin, legs flying, high over his head.

"So, birdling! You charge like a buck deer! Do not the silly girls teach manners?"

"Down! Down!" the peewee squealed, not frightened, not happy.

At that, one of the girls, the elder of the two, soberly offered to take the boy. She was taller than the other, her face pleasant and already beginning to look womanly. As she held out her hands for the four-year-old, her eyes sparkled.

"He is my brother. Let me have him and I will clear the others away. We should have noticed that you were a personage." She pointed to the turquoise ornament. "See," she told her mate. "He is a man." Then her eyes flashed mischief: "It is hard to tell nowadays who are our elders."

Salt handed over the struggling boy and was promptly butted from behind by another seeking his attention. This made it difficult for him to remove himself with dignity, but he managed it as a man should.

"Your beauty shines forth. May it remain with you," he blurted out, with the formality of an elderly uncle

speaking to a female relative. Behind him he heard suppressed laughter, and hurried his steps to escape from the
sound.

Now the sharp glare of the sun was screened by the
outer row of buildings and only a soft twilight penetrated
the street. The cave, in fact, seemed quite dark to anyone
entering from the cliff path. The air became chill and
stagnant. In winter, when clouds hung low and for days
no wind moved the stale air, the stench of people living
together within the cave penetrated everywhere.

He thought he heard his name called and wondered if
his mother would be here in the large plaza or at the
smaller one farther along. Then he heard the same voice
call his name again and his arm was grasped.

"We are the late ones again. What will our clan fathers
say this time?"

Salt turned to the speaker, and showed his annoyance
by frowning. The boy, of his own age, was called Star
Climber, and Salt considered this an inappropriate name.
The two had grown up together, played the same games,
and now they had been initiated into the men's society
together. Salt thought Star Climber was dull and slow.
He would never make a hunter because of his clumsiness
on the trail. He would never make a fighter because he
hung back when the play got rough. He would never make
a leader of the people because he believed everything he
was told and never knew what he believed himself. He
was a tiresome companion, but they had come all this way
together and nothing could be done about it. Salt walked
on without pausing.

"I suppose you were sleeping again," he said.

Star Climber smiled foolishly. "No one waked me when it was time. And what about you—I suppose you were doing something important."

For a moment Salt thought he would ignore the question, but presently he found himself explaining: "I was up before the sun and ran for two hours in the desert. Then I had other things to do—down there. I was just returning when I heard the call."

As they passed an open space between the buildings on their right, a narrow alley leading away into the deeper shadows of the inner cave, they heard the familiar sound of many turkeys gobbling. The boys paused and looked toward the sound.

"Should we go see what makes them talk?" Star Climber asked.

It was a foolish question which Salt did not answer. Star Climber often said things that left Salt wondering whether he realized that they were nonsense, or whether he said them only to tease. If they had been babes they might have followed the suggestion of going to look at the turkeys. Once, as children, they had gone to play with the carefully guarded birds, and had been soundly scolded. No one took it seriously then, since they knew no better, but such an escapade now would bring more than a scolding. Turkeys were called "divining birds," and were held in high regard. The flesh was never eaten and the birds were treated as if they were spokesmen and leaders of the people. When it was necessary to foretell some future event, certain priests consulted the turkeys, following a prescribed ceremony, and announced the findings in language which could be understood only with the greatest difficulty.

When a passer-by heard the turkeys talking among themselves, it was not seemly to stop and listen. Salt glared at his companion, who should have known better.

The street now led into a small plaza, where the sun again shone in full brightness. The buildings on the cliff-side had ended in a low parapet wall; women sat here in the sun, with their backs to a wall, their legs extending straight before them. Their dresses, of cotton, were fastened over the right shoulder, leaving the left shoulder free. Their hair was cut shoulder length and hung loose, for they were all wives and mothers. They were working from mounds of pottery clay, fashioning the moist earth into coils for the walls of various shapes of vessels. As they worked they chattered.

The women looked up as the boys approached, and Salt saw that his mother was one of the pottery workers. For a fleet second he watched her small strong hands add a slender coil of moist clay to the top of what would be a water jar and smooth the coil inside and out until a perfect joint had been made. Her fingers darted like swallows as they moved to the nearby basin of water, then to the clay, then back to the water. Surely there was no better potter in the White Rock Village!

His mother caught his look and smiled. "I believe you are awaited over there," she motioned with her lips.

Salt was aware that the guard at the ladder leading

down into the kiva was annoyed from too much waiting. Nevertheless, it was necessary to pause to look at his mother's flying fingers.

Another woman in the group spoke up. "Now that they have made a man of you, they'll not lose a chance to make you feel like a child. That's the way men are." The voice was half scolding, but it was not unpleasant. His mother's younger sister had spoken.

"As soon as you have finished, come to our house and eat." That was his mother again, her fingers never pausing.

"I leave you in happiness," he said, moving on.

"Go then in happiness," his mother answered, smiling fleetingly.

Star Climber had already descended the ladder into the kiva. The impatient guard was the very man who had called from the housetop, a little man with a large face. His chin, instead of coming to a point, looked like a round swelling in his neck, and his mouth usually hung half open as if from the weight of his baggy chin.

"When the Turquoise men are called, you will learn to come," the crier-guard said. The words seemed to come out of his nose, because his sagging lower lip hardly moved. He was called Stone Man. Salt placed his hand on the protruding ends of the ladder and step by step descended into the darkness.

He remembered again the man he had trailed at nightfall. He heard the man's low whistle, like the night hawk's, and the answering whistle. He had watched as a second figure emerged out of shadow, and he had crept closer to learn who the second person might be and to hear, if he could, what words passed. Then the scene seemed to dissolve, he lost track of the stealthy men—until he was grabbed from behind and sent spinning down the trail. He tried afterward to remember and to identify the voice of the speaker who had hissed at him: "Come this way again and your ears will be sliced off!"

Would someone, here in the kiva, reveal himself as one of those who met by darkness and by stealth? Would he be accused? And by whom? And of what?

Chapter 2

Voice of the Enemy

THE KIVA, a circular room without windows, could be entered only by the square opening in the roof, at once a smoke hole and a doorway. This was the meeting place for the men of the clan, but it was more than that. In it, Salt and boys of his own age, and boys before his time, were taught the art and skills of manhood. History and legend were told here, and the manner in which a man should stand before the world was proclaimed in many long speeches.

The interior was not entirely dark, since a fan of light came from above and a bed of red coals in the fire pit near the center of the room produced a faint glow, but it was so dim that Salt stood with one hand on the ladder until his eyes would save him from colliding with people. A knot of older men sat in a tight ring near the fire pit. They were passing a short-stemmed pottery pipe from one to another, each man puffing four times, then twice more, then handing it on.

As his eyes adjusted themselves and Salt could make his way to the seat assigned to him, his mind reached out to the men, his fathers, whose hands had worked so cleverly to lay together the stones for these walls. Men talked of kinship, but the laying up of a wall for one's children to use was a real thing. It bridged and held together those who had gone on and those who remained, in everlasting kinship. Salt always felt this when he looked upon the walls of his kiva.

Against the outer wall, at even intervals, six pillars reached to the top like six strong men and supported the pine beams on which the roof rested. In between these pillars ran a waist-high bench of stone. Those who sat on the bench were elevated above others, hence the seats were reserved for certain officers called "Speakers."

In the south wall of the kiva a square hole just above the floor brought fresh air. A slab of stone standing upright between the fresh-air opening and the fire pit deflected the current of air and caused it to circulate around the room and to create a draft for the fire. The walls were whitewashed frequently, as Salt and the other young men

knew, since they performed the work. Once a year, when
the clan leaders prepared for the Earth Renewing ceremony, the leader of the Masked God society repainted the
sacred symbols on the facing side of the stone pillars.

The men who had been smoking near the center of the
room presently rose and moved to their seats on the
benches. The talk would begin. Speaking in the kiva followed a regular procedure. Each of the principal officers
had a spokesman to talk for him. Sometimes a spokesman
came to a situation when he did not know what his man
wanted said, and in that case the meeting might break up,
or others might change the subject.

As the meeting began, Salt's attention wandered. From
thinking of ancient kinship with his fathers, his mind had
skipped to his morning run and he was again chasing a
rabbit through the sagebrush in the half-light. A man had
duties to perform, and meeting in the kiva was one of the
ways in which a man fulfilled himself. But the boy could
still remind the man that nothing in the world was as
pleasant as running free and alone in a great space, when
the stars are dimming and soft winds rise in the west! To
such an extent had Salt's thoughts strayed that he did not
hear at once the words directed at him, and did not see the
pointing hand.

"That boy will destroy us! You have heard me say this
before and I say it again!"

The speaker was rather short, with strong legs and
chest and long, powerful arms. His head seemed large
for the size of his body. He moved in bursts of speed, as
if something were ever on the point of getting away, and

he must ever be pouncing upon it. He spoke angrily, in a hoarse voice. This was Flute Man, who had no ceremonial office in the kiva but whose position was nonetheless important. As War Chief, or, as they sometimes said, Outside Chief, he was expected to see that men observed the fasts and purification rites required before they took part in important ceremonies. If such rules were disregarded, a ceremony might fail, and failure might mean that the corn would not grow, that men might become bewitched, or that enemies might steal their women and children. Men of the kiva were careful not to arouse Flute Man's suspicion or displeasure.

When Salt realized at last that all eyes were turned upon him, he stiffened. Flute Man belonged in his mother's family, yet he never seemed to be part of it. A man belonged to the house of his mother and his sisters, never to a house of his own. But Flute Man seemed to come and go according to some plan of his own. Salt could never remember a time when there had been any closeness between them. Older men were always quick to throw protecting arms around the younger boys of a family. They were the teachers, the sponsors, the go-betweens. Flute Man had been none of these, and Salt had never understood him. To be attacked by him was a double burden, since it was difficult to answer a relative.

"This is a serious thing, this talk against my son. We wait to hear the rest."

It was Shield, tall and stooping, who spoke. He used the term "son" in speaking of Salt, by which he meant that he regarded the boy as his young clansman. Shield,

an elder, was held in great respect and in his time had
filled many offices in clan and village.

Flute Man, the accuser, was not abashed at having his
words challenged by such a man as Shield.

"I speak of serious things, indeed. We expect our young
people to work in the cornfields, to learn what they need
to know, and to respect holy things. If you ask whether
this boy cares for such things, my duty requires me to tell
you he cares very little. When I go to the fields, he is
nowhere to be seen. But walk out on the desert down
there, beyond where our sacred stream vanished into the
earth—there you will find him, sitting on a rock idling
away his time. Or he will tell you he is hunting rabbits,
but I can say he rarely brings game home to his house. I
have watched, since that is part of my duty."

He paused to give his words effect, and a memory stirred
in Salt. He waited in a daze.

"As for learning what he will need to know when he
must go to war or help his people in time of trouble—I
can only say a boy sitting on a rock or running like a wolf
in the desert learns nothing to benefit himself, or his people. As for respecting holy things—you saw today how
he was last to come to our kiva meeting when, being a
young man, he should be among the earliest to arrive. Nor
is this the first time."

Shield listened to the end, then waited, allowing Flute
Man to continue further if he desired. When nothing more
came, the thin old man lifted his long face, framed by
straggling ends of graying hair, and gazed long at the
accused boy.

"Son," the tone was gentle, "we will give you permission to talk, if you wish it. What can you say in answer to our brother? As he says, these are serious matters."

Salt had never before been invited to speak in the kiva; seldom was a young man so asked. His feelings came up in a lump as he glanced at the set faces before him. Only Flute Man stared back. The others regarded the earth at their feet and indicated neither favor nor disfavor. To speak out forcefully and win the minds of men—that was the thing any boy might dream about from his first kiva meeting. How different, when the time came! He looked again at the lowered heads and wondered if it would not be wiser to hold his tongue and not risk offending his elders. Perhaps he would have chosen the latter course if Climbing Star, seated next to him, had not nudged him and hissed: "Better not speak! Flute Man is watching you!"

The cautioning words stung Salt. He must speak.

"Flute Man, my uncle, knows that our corn grows badly." Courtesy was prized by his people as one of the first virtues, and Salt was careful to show courtesy by word and tone. "Each year it gets worse. I spoke of this. I said our people should move their fields from the land above, where there are many rocks and no water, and plant them down there in the canyon. The spring water disappears into the earth just where the canyon opens and grows wide. The sagebrush is thick at that place and willows grow there also, drinking up the water. When I spoke of this, he answered that such things are not for me to think about. So I made a place in the sagebrush—I chopped it away and dug it out. Then I planted corn there. It is now three times as high as the corn in the upper fields. I think my uncle does not like this."

Several of the listening men sat back and looked at the boy. He could hear the quick sucking in of breath. Flute Man called out. "You see! Just hear how he talks!" His face was shining with a victor's glee. "His own words condemn him."

Shield persisted in his gentle voice: "You know, boy, that our fields above were laid out by our fathers, and that is where we plant. The ground below has never been consecrated. Who goes there, goes in peril."

"Uncle, I knew of that. Yet, I knew how in our family field every year we have less corn, hardly enough to eat; none to store for the bad year when all corn will fail. I think that bad year will come soon."

Confirming voices sounded around the room. "The boy says well. This is a true thing."

Flute Man was quick to interrupt the agreeing tones.

"Is a boy to set aside our accepted way of living? I warned you he does not respect holy things. Now you hear for yourselves. The corn he planted will have to be pulled up. Otherwise, who knows what may befall our people. The very spring by which we live may fail us. Destroy the corn, I say, then consider what to do with him. For something must be done."

Shield once more pressed into the discussion. "I think we will first look at the boy's corn before we pull it up. Others say the bad year might be coming soon. I agree. Each year our sacred spring gives a smaller stream of water, as we all know. When this boy was an infant, you could hear the water roar as it came down from the mountain wall. Now you have to listen carefully on the quietest night to hear it from up here. What will happen to these people when the water is gone?"

Salt, listening, suddenly heard the voice again, and excitement burned in his eyes. The voice was speaking, not about the planting of corn. It was nighttime, and out of the shadow it hissed, "Come this way again—" Salt looked away, fearful that his burning eyes would give him away. Better that he say no more.

Flute Man, showing unhappiness, rose to his feet. Speakers did not rise except on formal occasions, but Flute Man was too excited to think about that. "This cannot be! The boy will destroy us!" He looked challengingly from face to face until he had surveyed every man in the kiva.

At that point an aged blind man, who sat in the back row with Salt and the newly initiated men, spoke up in the quaver of the ancient.

"I can't see Flute Man but I know he is looking at me. His eyes poke at me like willow sticks. I will only ask him if he is a priest to decide where we may plant."

Flute Man, of course, was not a priest, and the remark fetched a sprinkling of laughter.

At that point, one of the speakers slid from his place on the high bench. He was a stout man, of a serious expression, as was proper in one of his position. His graying hair was tied down with a band of red woven stuff that circled his head. They called him Day Singer.

"I think the boy should go now. We will take this into our thoughts. Surely a strange thing has happened and must be answered in some fashion." In that there was agreement.

Salt hurried up the ladder when told that he could go, and once he reached the open air his pent-up breath burst from him. Something surely was happening, something beyond anything he had ever imagined. Who were these men who had met in stealth? Who, besides this one whose name he now knew?

Chapter 3

Face to Face

D ARKNESS crept up the canyon wall like flood waters rising against the banks of a stream. By the time the sun crossed the arc of sky above the towering rock walls, the flood of shadow was at the brim. At that moment, a chilling wind blew into the cave of White Rock Village.

When Salt stepped from the ladder to the roof of the kiva and found that he had missed the sun, it was as if a friend had gone ahead without waiting. He stood at the edge of the little plaza and gazed upward. Stars were already visible in the blue depths above. A nighthawk hurtled through the air, startling the silence. The cave was a lonely place at the moment between daylight and darkness.

His mother had gone with the warmth of the day. He paused near where she and the other women had worked in the sun. Evening chill shook him; then he was hungry.

From the darkening canyon, he turned to the still darker cave. Cooking fires glowed on roof terraces and threw feeble shadows on house and cave walls. Cedarwood gave off no smoke when it burned, but it left a sweet stinging odor in the air.

He climbed a short ladder to one terrace, crossed to a shadowed wall, climbed a steeper ladder, then stood in firelight. A voice called.

"Here is our youngest father returning from the council. He has discovered that hunger grows faster than wisdom."

It was his mother's youngest sister, Shell Woman, laughing as always. He did not mind being chided by her. It brought a feeling of well-being.

"We kept the pot near the fire all afternoon. Is the talking finished?"

His mother had stepped to his side and he could see the firelight glow in her searching eyes. His head was already above hers.

"Ah, no," she continued before he spoke. "You left before the others. And you are troubled."

The people called her Becoming Day, and she had the trick of knowing when he was tired or sick or downcast. After she satisfied herself with a look, she lost no time preparing a remedy.

"Food first," she ordered. "Sit, and I will bring it to you."

The warm food, tasting fragrantly of the sage his mother cooked with the meat, brought a certain peace. Whatever the voices in the kiva might be saying, here for a moment was forgetfulness. The glowing embers of the cooking fire gave light and comfort. Let Flute Man talk in shadow and anger; it was of no concern here. He gathered his feet close under and sat firm on a mound of mountain-goat skin.

A lesser figure moved away from the fire glow, then merged in shadow. His name was called softly, but not the name his elders called him by. It was a secret name, used only by his younger sister.

"Muddy-O" was the whispered sound. And hearing it, he smiled in the secret shadow.

It was as if a bright light burst upon him, as when the sun suddenly shoots from behind a thundercloud and fashions a new landscape. It was a name of laughter and games, a name that went with leaping from stone to stone, of plunging into the cool waters that flowed at the bottom of the canyon. On one such day, he being a boy of ten and his sister a child of six years, they had played until exhaustion caught up with them and they lay down at the mossy edge of the canyon stream. First they lay and told stories about the beasts of earth and sky—idle caricatures of the stories their elders told in high seriousness. The stories grew drowsier, and presently they both slept. When Salt awoke (at the time he was called simply the Youngest Boy), it was to a sound of laughter. He lay a moment to get his wits together, fearing that he had slept too long. Then quickly he put his hands to his itching face and found that he had been plastered with mud! His sister, by then, was already out of range and as she danced away, leaping up the trail to the cave village, she chanted, "Brother has a mud face! Brother has a mud face!"

He smiled in the shadows, remembering how the words echoed back at him from the canyon walls. By the time he reached the village, running to catch his taunting sister when he should have stopped to wash, the name "Mud Face" was tossed back at him from every household.

Only his sister still remembered, but she had softened her conquest with the years.

"Muddy-O" was the sound he heard.

Young people grew up early in the Village of the White Rocks. His sister, Morning Shell, at eleven, was already a cook, a potter and a weaver of sorts. A woman of the household.

She came quite close before she spoke further.

"Our mother did not speak of this. She wanted you to eat first. But there is to be trouble. Word has come from the kiva that you did some bad thing, and that you will be punished. I did not believe it, my brother. How can they punish you in that case?"

"They will not ask what you believe, little mustard seed, though I am happy to hear you speak in my favor."

"What will they do, and why do they say you have done a bad thing?"

"You might agree with them if I told you. Then I would have no one to talk for me."

"You speak in fun. Our mother will speak out for you. But you must tell me."

"This much I tell you truly. I know what is said against me, but my accuser says one thing and means something else. Only time will answer the riddle."

The answer did not satisfy the girl, who moaned softly in the darkness. Salt had to stare hard at the shadowy form at his side to be sure it was his child sister, she sounded so like a woman full grown.

"They will send the masked gods to whip you with rawhide knots. Blood will run from your skin. I see it, Brother! You must go away!"

He reached across and touched her arm. "You frighten yourself—"

Forms had appeared above the parapet. Now they were moving forms, approaching the fire. He twisted his sister's shoulder to turn her toward the fire.

"See, these are not masked gods. They are—"

His sister trembled under his hand.

First came Eldest Woman, his mother's mother, who lived alone in the Chief's Tower, with only a granddaughter to cook for her. Age and shortness of breath had slowed her, but she still climbed ladders and busied herself in the village. They could hear her mighty gasps as she threw her short legs over the parapet. Next to come was Shield, tall and stooped, who had questioned Flute Man in the kiva. Then came the man wearing the red woven band around his head, the one called Day Singer. Last of all to scramble out of the shadow into the firelight, Flute Man himself.

*   *   *   *   *

All sat in the room, their forms imperfectly revealed in the light of a pinon torch whose resins smoked and sputtered. Only the Eldest Woman showed clearly, since the flame was held near her to help her in her half-blindness. Once she had been fat, then she had wasted, and folds of skin now hung loosely under her chin. The brown scalp showed in patches through the thin mat of gray hair. She spoke first.

"I want to know what is being said about my grandson. If it is idle talk, it must stop. Well, who waits? Speak up!"

Flute Man thrust his large head forward into the light.

"It is not what people are saying, Grandmother, but what the boy himself says. Call upon him to speak."

"In due time," the ancient one answered. "It is reported that you accuse the boy of placing a curse on his people. If you have a reason, I came to hear it."

Flute Man was not tall, but when he arose his head almost touched the low ceiling. A robe of rabbit's wool was thrown over his left shoulder, leaving his right arm free to gesture. The flaring torch was a bright spark in his wild eyes.

Salt, looking up at the speaker, saw the angry eyes. But he also saw the tuft of eagle feathers hanging from the center beam. This would keep evil from the room, he thought, and no harm would come to him. That, at least, was what the old people believed; but one could not always count on it. An accident could befall an unlucky person.

"These men were present." Flute Man motioned into the shadows. "They know what was said."

Salt felt his breath rise and fall. Now he was tempted

to speak and put an end to this wasting of words; now he would hold his tongue. In his indecision, he waited and heard Flute Man repeat again the blind and ugly words he had uttered in the kiva.

"If our sacred spring dries up entirely, this witless boy will be the cause, since he goes against the ways of our people."

The speaker stared at each shadowy figure in turn. Then when his eyes came to Eldest Woman, he drew back and presently was seated again.

"Well!" Impatience exploded in the clan mother's single word. "Who else will speak?"

The boy's face grew hot, but still he held back. Eldest Woman had always been ancient in Salt's memory. She had a longer name, but no one spoke it. Other women might visit his mother and smile upon her family. Not this mother of mothers, as older women were sometimes called. On the rare occasions when children encountered her in the plaza or on the trail, her eyes were far away and took no notice of what laughter, fear or sorrow might be in the young faces she encountered. To speak in her presence, to risk her rebuke, was a fearful thing. As the silence endured, Salt grew tense; then, gratefully, he saw Shield rising out of the shadows. The pressure in his chest at once escaped in a great sigh that the clan mother heard. She raised one ragged eyebrow in his direction, but Salt was too preoccupied to notice.

Shield talked in wispy, dry tones. "We are children of the Turquoise Clan gathered here. We dwell all in the same house. We know that beyond our walls other clans-

men watch us jealously. Our legends tell us that Turquoise
men were the first to occupy the Village of the White
Rocks. As the first, we were the most powerful. It was for
us to decide who might live in the village and who might
not."

Shield did not speak hurriedly. He let each sentence
linger before starting another. His stooped figure fitted
just under the ceiling, so that his voice seemed to cling to
the yellow pine beams.

"Our power is not what it was. Our numbers grow less.
Then, as you know, the Holy One, our true leader, moved
out of our village and lives alone. I speak no more of
that, but it is a certainty that since that day of misfortune
our strength has been drying up like a field without water.
Beyond our walls, people watch. They are hungry. They
may be our younger children, but they sharpen their flint
knives for our throats. Take care that our own actions do
not split us apart and leave us ready for those knives."

The speaker halted on a tone of uncertainty, then
seemed to decide against saying more. Cautiously he moved
backward until he found his place in the shadows.

Eldest Woman frowned. "Shield talks strangely. Who
is splitting us apart?"

Shield rose to his feet again, but did not move forward
into the flickering light. He was a voice without form.

"The spring in the canyon is life-giver to us all. Without
the water, the Village of the White Rocks would be filled
with our bleached bones. When a speaker in the kiva blames
a Turquoise man for the failing spring, by morning every
child in the village will point at that man. Our kiva talks

are supposed to be kept within the kiva, but everyone knows that stones have ears. Such a story will grow, until it is claimed that our clan itself is at fault—and thus our enemies, the envious ones of our village, will be made bolder."

Flute Man came forward into the light, impatient to answer Shield, but Eldest Woman held him back with a gesture.

"Do you still insist that this grandson, who wears the badge of a Turquoise man, is destroying our spring?"

Salt moved his hand in the dark, feeling for the turquoise ornament. The elders had told him at the time of his initiation that the touch of that stone would drive fear out of a true Turquoise man. In time of danger, it would protect him from harm; it would insure a full and happy life. For was not the turquoise the gift of the blue sky, where the Sun Father traveled? Sun Old Man, he was also called. The people prayed to him at his rising, they prayed to him when he stood still at midday, and again when he entered his evening house. Turquoise reminded a man of the peace that dwelt in the sky. It said to the mind, Behold, here is the way to live, at peace with your brothers!

Fingering the blue stone, Salt felt the turmoil subside in his breast. Let Flute Man say what he would!

His thoughts strayed and he did not follow closely on Flute Man's opening words. What he finally heard drove thoughts of peace from his mind and left him shivering. It was difficult, he was learning, to hold a thing fast in his thinking.

"—and that is why I say he is a meddling child and

must be corrected. What matter, O Grandmother, whether the Turquoise Clan be split asunder by what happens among us, if our entire Seven Clans are to be destroyed? Do you wish us to bind up our mouths while this impure child remains among us, bringing us to shame and destruction?"

"I've heard enough! Let the boy speak. You, Grandson! Come where I can see your face. Now, tell me if you understand what has been said against you, and how you answer."

The slender boy stood straight before his elders. His breathing rose and fell, and he hardly knew at first whether any words would come.

"I understand it well, my Grandmother. My mother's youngest brother wants our people to plant corn where there is no water. He says the corn land is the high land. Yet he knows, even as I know, that up there the corn plants are weaker each year and bear fewer ears. I think in the days of our elders more rain fell on the high land. The stream beds are there still, but now they are dry. It looks as though those streams have been dry a long time—"

Eldest Woman muttered to herself, but loud enough to be heard: "The boy obviously uses his eyes. We had mighty rains in my childhood. Continue!" she called out, aware of her interruption.

"With my digging stick I made a deep hole, and the earth was dry to the depth of my stick. I mean no disrespect, but I say it is better to plant our corn down in the canyon where the water from the spring sinks into the ground.

"But that is not all I understand—" The boy turned suddenly in the direction of Flute Man.

"Now you have heard him!" the angry accuser interrupted. "This is no simple child."

"Be quiet, you! I wish to hear him."

Salt breathed deeply for strength. "My uncle speaks of the corn I planted below. He shames me before others. He wishes you not to listen to me, not to believe me. Because I know something about him. This he knows—"

"I warn you, you mud-faced child! Watch your tongue!"

"He talks in dark corners with men whose faces I could not see—but I can name one."

Eldest Woman gasped. "Child—" she began.

Salt rushed on. The words were crowding for utterance and he must say them before his breath failed.

"My uncle knows what I saw—and he would silence me. He talks to the one we call Dark Dealer—"

Flute Man hurled himself against the boy, crying, "A knife! A knife! I'll cut out his black tongue!"

As they crashed to the floor, Salt felt sharp fingers at his throat. He lashed out with hands and feet, but still the clawing fingers squeezed. He struck blindly.

Then his throat was suddenly free. The weight lifted from his body.

It was the stocky, gray-haired Day Singer who had plunged in and grasped Flute Man by the hair.

Then there was silence, save for the harsh gasping breath that seemed to fill the place. Salt sat cross-legged in the middle of the room, his heart pounding at his ribs.

Eldest Woman, having reflected on what she had heard and seen, spoke at last. She looked at Flute Man.

"Now you must leave." Her voice, flat and cold, was not accusing. "We will talk again of this. Shield and Day Singer I ask to stay."

Flute Man was enraged. "You will listen to this boy's lies. I insist on hearing him out!"

"You will go," Eldest Woman replied and did not even glance up.

As Flute Man turned, he kicked out at Salt, but the blow fell short. Day Singer had nudged him with his shoulder enough to throw him off balance. They heard him on the roof terrace a moment later. He had bumped against a shadowed form.

"O you snooping women! Get to your beds!"

A silence fell upon the room again. Once the commotion had ceased, the pinon torch burned quietly.

The boy remained cross-legged in the center of the room, waiting. He did not regret what he had said; his eyes had not deceived him. But he was not so long removed from childhood as to forget how grown people often treated the words of a young person. They would ask him how he knew. Was he sure? Did he realize what he was saying? He waited.

At last Eldest Woman sighed, as one who comes from a deep sleep.

"The Dark Dealer has killed men. Everyone speaks of it."

Salt knew this and said nothing.

"It is known that he talks to the Cloud People—the Dead. He has the power of witchcraft."

This also Salt knew, and he said nothing.

"He is the only man in all the village who dares to look into a spring when the sun stands at the high point of the day. And we know why he can do that and not be stricken with a blank mind. Only one man stands against the Dark Dealer. Him we call the Holy One. Shield and Day Singer know why the Holy One lives in a cave by himself, and there's no need to tell that story now."

Eldest Woman had been talking, as if to herself, gazing straight ahead. Now she looked down at Salt squatting on the floor.

The tuft of eagle feathers hanging overhead turned halfway in a draft of air, then turned back, like something alive. Would those feathers still protect him, or would he be one of the unlucky ones?

"If Flute Man has been talking to Dark Dealer, it was wrong of you, child, to speak of it when Flute Man was here among us. Now you have put him on his guard and we may not find out what scheme they are plotting until it is too late."

She fell silent but all knew she would speak again. Her thoughts were traveling afar, but would return.

"What it is to be, we will know in time. I am not thinking about that now. I am thinking of how we will protect you. Trouble may fall on you first, before anything else is tried. To protect you, we must take your manhood badge away from you. That is my thought."

Salt, startled by the words, clutched the turquoise pendant.

"The kiva must be asked to reverse the ceremony which made you a man. As a child, no one will touch you, for Sun Old Man is the special protector of children. Even Dark Dealer knows that. The village people will force him to respect that much of our law."

Salt rose to his knees, and stayed there. His eyes urged the right to speak.

"What you are saying—surely this cannot be. I am not afraid. The stone will protect me, as it protects all Turquoise men. Without it, as you say, I would be a child again; and what can a child do for his people! Let me remain a man, my Grandmother, and I will show you how I can protect us all!"

The voice of Eldest Woman grew sharp and crisp.

"Now you are showing us that you are indeed a child. You will protect us! Do you think it not possible for your elders to take care of themselves, and of you as well? We will talk no more of this. Remove the stone from his neck. I am going to bed. Tomorrow make the announcement."

And that night the boy Salt did indeed become a child again. In the lowermost room where he went to sleep, in utter darkness, his tears poured over his hands as he held them to his mouth to stifle his own outcries. He shuddered, but made no sound. The hours went by, shrouded in darkness, and in time his limbs began to slacken and stretch their length.

At the very end of that night, almost as sleep caught him, a last moment of alertness held him fast. In that moment came a sound which, as a very young child, he had often heard. Or was it a sound? Like stones dropping, one by one, into a hole of deep water. Like the beat of a very distant drum. Or was it only tears dropping from his eyes upon the packed earth floor? His eyes by then were quite dry, but still he heard the throb of something, perhaps the very heart of the earth itself.

Chapter 4

The Owl's Claw

WHEN Flute Man left the house of Salt's mother, he scrambled over parapet, ladder, and roof until he reached the dark inner street of the cliff village. There, safely in shadow, he waited. No one moved. No sounds came. Still he waited.

When he moved finally, no one could have said he moved. He simply became one with the shadow and was no longer there.

Staying within the deep shadows, he hurried, slipping through the village until he reached the high place, where the log ladder led downward. Quickly he descended, his feet finding the notches unerringly. Halfway down the cliff, he paused again. Waited and listened. Then he followed a ledge of rock which went, not downward as the villagers went when they descended into the canyon, but off to his left, seemingly into the void. The ledge was only the width of a moccasined foot. Then presently there was no ledge at all, only toe- and handholds in the solid rock. Flute Man moved more slowly, feeling each grappling place, pulling himself upward over the waiting emptiness of the canyon. He breathed without effort, seeming to feel neither fear nor uncertainty. At last he pulled himself over the edge and into a narrow crack in the cliff. With a last flip of his feet, he disappeared into the rock.

In the blackness, after he had crawled a body's length, he could feel himself descending. He rose to his knees, then stood at full height. It was a lesser cave, lying just below the great cave of the village.

He moved no further, for just as he got to his feet the point of a flint knife lodged against his ribs. A voice growled in his ear.

"Are you alone?"

"Of course, fool!"

"Then who saw you come?"

"Worse-than-fool! No one saw me."

Flute Man was pushed roughly forward into the darkness and the voice behind him rasped, "Save your brave words for the one in there."

For a moment, unbalanced in the utter darkness, Flute

Man struck against sharp rocks and in the black record
of his mind vowed that he would repay the guard. The
power would be his someday, and not far off, to repay all
who had abused him.

A low fire burning in the pit threw a vague and waver-
ing light over the faces of three seated men. The man,
Dark Dealer, with two others sat in the kiva of the Spider
Clan.

Dark Dealer was not an old man, yet he occupied a
place of leadership which normally fell to only the oldest
men in a clan. Power and position usually came to men
late in life, after they had survived the accidents of existence and had arrived at wisdom and tolerance. Dark Dealer
was the youngest son of a family which, before him, had
not been noted for wisdom or bravery. If he had gone the
normal course, his voice would never have been heard in
the kiva meeting, and if he had risen to speak none would
have listened.

But his life had not taken the usual course. It was ru-
mored that at his birth, when he was carried outdoors to
be presented to the sun, a dark cloud suddenly appeared
and remained over the sun until the godparents and infant
returned to the house. He was taken out a second day, and
again a cloud covered the sun. On a third occasion, it was
the same. And when it happened even on a fourth attempt,
the godparents refused to have anything more to do with
the child. Thus, he was never presented to the sun and,
in a manner of speaking, was never properly brought into

life. That was the rumor, but doubtless like all rumors it had grown with the telling.

People also remembered that when Dark Dealer came up for initiation and one of the masked figures stepped forward to whip him across the back with a willow sapling, in token of his acceptance into the clan, the sapling broke in the masked figure's hand and the boy was never touched. Later, people pointed to this as a sign that the boy possessed special powers. Not even the masked impersonator of one of the supernatural people could touch him.

Then came the time when the office of War Chief in the Spider Clan was to be filled. The prior War Chief, as he lay dying, named as his successor a nephew whom he had been training for years. But this nephew, even before the ceremony could be performed which would accomplish his chieftainship, fell over a cliff and broke his neck. In such a situation, the next male relative in the mother's line was usually chosen. But when a candidate had been selected in this instance and announcement of the coming ceremony was made, the candidate was struck by lightning as he went out to gather pinon nuts. The clansmen hesitated to name a third candidate, but while they hesitated Dark Dealer offered himself and was able to prove that his mother's family was distantly related to the late War Chief.

So began his climb to power. The very name, Dark Dealer, was first used then, but as only a whisper passing to and fro. Until hearing of it, he proclaimed it as his own. He even laughed about it.

"The people will remember that name. We'll make it stand for something," he told his clansmen in the kiva. They laughed with him, but none knew for sure whether it was a thing to laugh about, or not.

The War Chief, it was believed, had control over the enemy. His was the power to protect his people against the spirits of enemies slain in battle. His also was the power, it was said, to control the actions of the dead, and to thrust witches away from the people. These were dangerous tasks, but they must be performed by someone. The War Chief had never been an important office in the clan—until Dark Dealer came along and made it so. The clan was led nominally by an old man, Dawn Child, who bore the title of Sun Watcher. This was a position of unusual holiness, since the person in it had the duty of keeping the calendar and of naming the days of important ceremonies. To miscalculate in reckoning these propitious dates might destroy the crops, the very people themselves.

Of him, Dark Dealer said: "Let this old man watch the rocks where the sun passes in his journeys, and let him make the proper prayer sticks for offerings. But look to me; I will make our Spider Clan powerful. It is for Spider Clan men to decide who may live in the Village of the White Rocks. The Turquoise Clan has held this power too long. We live here only by their good will, and who knows when our children may be driven over the cliff? We have a duty to our children to make ourselves powerful. Does any man disagree?"

And none disagreed.

So, through many twistings and turnings, schemes, and

secret meetings, Flute Man, who was not a man of power, but who had his own ambitions within the Turquoise Clan, came to the kiva of the Spider Clan.

Like all other kivas, this one had a daylight entrance through a hole in the roof. A ladder led down into it and anyone could see who came and went by the ladder. But there was also a secret entrance, up the face of the cliff, through a crack in the rock which in daylight was hardly visible from below, then through a narrow cave and the ventilator shaft which led from the cave into the kiva.

Flute Man crawled into the ventilator shaft, and waited. He was still angry with the guard who had pushed him, but not so angry as to forget caution. He crawled silently forward, until by the dim light in the fire pit he could observe who was present. When he satisfied himself that Dark Dealer was alone with his two assistants, he made the chipping sound of a chipmunk. Then waited again.

Inside the kiva, the men moved like machines set in motion by a spring. Dark Dealer arose at once and held up his hand, demanding caution. One of the assistants went to the ladder and climbed out on the roof. The second assistant stopped at the foot of the ladder and took a position where he could watch the man above. Dark Dealer then dropped his hand to his side.

"You risk us all, coming thus without forewarning. I have a flint knife for anyone who ruins our plans." Dark Dealer's voice was low, scarcely audible, yet there was energy in what he said.

Flute Man felt the sting. "When knives are used, mine will not be idle."

The two men were about of the same height, but Dark Dealer was the more powerful. His shoulders and arms were better muscled and his hands were larger. In grappling with a man, he could surely break an arm or a windpipe. Knowing his strength, Dark Dealer said no more, but smiled.

"My sister's youngest boy, that meddler Salt, has been talking with Eldest Woman."

"Well, continue! What did he say?"

Flute Man had come to Dark Dealer's kiva with a purpose, and not merely to report a conversation. That was why, meeting Dark Dealer's gaze squarely, he lied, saying: "The boy accused you of planning to destroy Turquoise Clan."

"How does he say this? What does he know?" The questioner's eyes blazed sharply.

"He makes wild guesses, hoping to win attention. He knows nothing. But he talks, and he must be stopped."

"He'll be stopped—but I want to know why he talks. A child does not speak unless he sees something. Has he seen you climb the cliff up here?"

"He said he saw—but he was lying."

Dark Dealer moved quickly and with one powerful hand grasped the other by the throat.

"It's as I thought. That night you met me at the edge of the village—and said you had to go back. The boy trailed you! So! A child, for all your talk, is smarter than you are. You want to know our plans? You want to take part in them? Then I tell you what you must do. Destroy this boy! Get him out of my way. If you do that without getting caught in a trap, come back, and I will tell you how you can help, and what part you will play."

A shove of the powerful hand sent Flute Man stumbling across the room, until he collapsed against the wall. Dark Dealer sprang forward and stood over him, threatening to seize him once more.

"Only remember. If you are caught, the blame is yours. I will say I know nothing of what you do. I have ears everywhere; if you talk, you will never talk again."

In shame, Flute Man arose. In shame, he moved away from the hurler of threats and toward the ventilator shaft. This was a square opening, no wider than a man's shoulders, placed at the level of the floor. It brought in fresh air for the fire and kept the kiva sweet-smelling.

"You will need help," Dark Dealer spoke up in softer tones. "We want no failure in what you do. I give you this owl's claw to hide on your person. It will protect you against witching powers and give you the cunning to do what must be done."

Flute Man glanced with horror at the sharp claw nestled in a ball of feathers. He backed away.

"This I cannot do. You know our people stone to death any man who is found bearing any part of an owl. Such help is not needed to carry out this little task. I will find pleasure in it, I assure you."

"Take it, I say!"

"It isn't needed. Wait and see."

"You refuse? Too bad, then, because I have decided you can't leave here without it. Too much is at stake. Fire Striker!"

At the sound of his name, the man at the foot of the ladder moved toward the two.

"Is all clear up above?" Dark Dealer asked.

"The short-legged one has given no signal."

"Go up and tell him to be watchful. I will need your help for a minute."

"What will you do?" Alarm entered Flute Man's voice. "We are friends together in this. You will need my help before you finish."

"I decide what help I need. Just now I have decided that I can manage without you. In the morning they will find you at the bottom of the cliff."

Flute Man dived headfirst toward the ventilator shaft. But not quickly enough. He was seized around the knees and brought to the earth-packed floor. After a brief tussle he lay still.

The one called Fire Striker was back from the ladder and ready to take a hand. "How will we do it?" the man asked.

"Wait until this one gets his breath again. Then I'll ask him once more which way he chooses."

But Flute Man did not have to wait. He had heard the words and was ready to speak.

"Give me the owl's claw. I can see your plan is best. When the task is finished, I will return it."

"When the task is finished, yes. Then we will talk again. Do not come here until you have completed it. The guard out there will be watching."

Flute Man squirmed his way through the air shaft. A

moment later he could be heard quarreling with the guard in the cave.

Dark Dealer smiled. "In this way," he told his companion at the fire pit, "we get rid of one, maybe two. With good planning it may be two. Spread the word that Flute Man carries the owl's claw. That will set people to watching him—and when he strikes, they will also be ready to strike."

Chapter 5

Nothing Is Built on Fear

THE MAN called the Holy One lived alone in his rock shelter high above the great cave of the village. Sometimes, looking up, people could see him hopping around like a child at play. "See Grandfather Grasshopper," mothers told their children.

And the same mothers would say to each other, out of hearing of their children: "The fool will fall and break his neck. Not that it would make any difference, since he has deserted us."

Men with serious village problems frequently went up to ask his advice, but they never knew how they would be received. At times they found him crawling around on all fours, and for every question they asked, his only answer was to bark, doglike. At other times he curled up like a bear in hibernation, and no amount of coaxing would cause him to heed their talk. On still other occasions he stood on the rock ledge in front of his cave house and threw stones at anyone trying to climb the steep trail to his abode. When he did respond to questions, and this was a rare occasion, his talk was so difficult that the men spent days in the kiva afterward trying to unravel his words. He resorted to backward talk—a trick of saying the opposite of what he meant. In order to understand his true meaning, the men had to remember the exact wording of the questions they asked and the answers he gave.

No one could have told his age in years, since the people of those times were not so much concerned with the passage of years as they were with the happenings of nature which were encompassed in a man's lifetime. Some could remember back to an early autumn when many families from the Village of the White Rocks were trapped and frozen to death in an unseasonable blizzard which struck while they were gathering pinon nuts. Even farther back in memory was the winter when a heavy wet snow fell, then froze sharply, and a great ledge of rock broke from the opposite cliff and crashed to the canyon bottom with a roar that seemed to shatter the world. Two little girls were crushed at the spring and the spring itself was almost destroyed.

The Holy One had lived through those and many other

dire events. His long, unkempt hair was almost white.
Even his skin seemed bleached, when he sat opposite a
younger tribesman. The deer-hide garments he wore,
black and shiny with grime, appeared to be as ancient as he.
He had never been a large man, but the years had wasted
him until the bones of his face and his limbs looked too big
for the skin that stretched over them. His eyes alone
looked keen and ageless—but that was when he was by
himself, gazing off across the world of broken rock and
black pine headlands. When people came from below to
complain of things in the village, most likely his eyes
would roll until only the whites showed, or he would
simply close them and pucker up his face like the pumpkin
slices the people dried on their roof tops.

They called him the Holy One because it was thought
that he had been touched by the spirits of the other world
—hence, no longer entirely a part of the world of men.
He was entitled, therefore, to a special kind of respect
by men.

That morning as the old man watched the boy Salt
scramble upward over the path of loose rocks, he indulged
in no strange antics and no stone-throwing. But he moved
away from the rock on which he had been sitting in plain
view of the village, and retreated into his cave. There Salt
found him, his eyes looking up brightly.

It was a morning when the air over the mountains hung
clear and tender. Smoke rising from a cooking fire
ascended in a straight line until it finally dissolved high
up against the arching sky. Meadow larks called clearly
and the drumming sound of doves came up from the can-

yon. A pine squirrel ran his long trill with the chirping sounds at the end. Each stir of air brought a smell of sage and juniper, commingled as one scent.

"May you have happiness today, Grandfather," the boy greeted.

"Peace to you, boy." The old man pointed to a flat rock slightly below his own.

"Here you can sit and look out upon the world, and watch who comes up the trail. Also, it is easier to talk when another is not watching your face."

Salt's eyes widened in surprise. The old man seemed to know that he had come to talk of difficult things.

"You never come unless you have serious problems to solve," the Holy One said, as if the boy had expressed his surprise aloud. "Anyhow, your turquoise badge is missing and that troubles you. So speak, boy. No one will stop you or accuse you."

"You know what was said, then? You know what happened?"

"I only know what comes drifting to me on the wind."

It was often said that nothing happened in the cliff village that was not reported in full to the Eagle's Nest, as the Holy One's cave was called.

For a long time after Salt had finished his story, beginning with the scene in the kiva, and while the sun climbed midway up the morning sky, the old man made no comment. Once Salt looked back over his shoulder to assure himself that his listener had not fallen asleep. When he found the ancient eyes burning fiercely, he looked away quickly.

"My people think my mind is gone," the old one said finally.

The boy was silent, ashamed to admit that the village talked of this.

"It surprises me that I have my senses still. I know how it is down there. They tell lies. They meet in secret. I am old, but I am still Chief, and some don't like that."

"Eldest Woman said I talked too big. But maybe I could help a little, if I had my turquoise badge."

Salt was surprised to hear the old man laugh—a dry cackling sound.

"We are captives, you and I. To protect you, they take away your badge. For my own protection, I leap around like a goat. We won't be touched while we are as we are, but it has its disadvantages. It is a game to play while we wait, and you must understand that."

"That is what I don't understand, Grandfather. What do we wait for?"

"For the enemy to show who he is, and how he intends to move."

"The enemy has already shown himself."

"Flute Man? Yes, I have known that for some time. Dark Dealer is his master, as I also know. But who else? There are others moving around down there. Stories come up to me."

"I am ashamed to be a child again."

"Ah, no doubt. You are young and want to grow fast. Do you know what—I am ashamed, even in my age when I should outgrow such things, I am ashamed to act like an old fool! It's a game. But do you know why I do it?"

"To wait, you said."

"Yes. But if I lived down there, with those lies and those secret meetings, I would forget my duty. You know how our people say that the Chief should be pure of heart, never become angry. He works for peace. Yes. But if I were down there, I might take my knife or my club and destroy these troublemakers."

"Somebody will have to do it, I think."

"The people will do it, once they know."

"They will poison the minds of the people."

"You think things out. And so I am sure you will be a great leader of the people someday. Also that is why I talk to you freely, and someday may depend on you. But these men are not strong enough to win the people over. They will use fear if they can. They will try to make the people afraid of me, or of you, or of anyone who is trusted by the people. A few weak ones will accept fear as a way of action—and out of fear they may use knives and spill blood. But nothing is built on fear, and they will pass away."

"I believe this, Grandfather. But as a child, I have no part in anything. How long will it be?"

The sun stood in his midday house, where he pauses to catch his breath after the long climb up the morning sky. It was the time when a prayer is said and no one stays out of doors or in the full glare of the sun if he can avoid it. Salt waited until the old man raised his head again.

"We have talked a long time, yet there is still much that must be said another time. Only I will say this, Grandson. Eldest Woman acted in her right and her power in returning you to childhood. She is your godmother. She presented you to the sun at your birth hour. So she is responsible for you and she did this to protect you. But there is a way to win back your manhood badge."

"That is what I want! Only tell me!"

"I will set you a task. Maybe there will be a second task after that."

"Good. I will perform anything you say."

"These will not be easy tasks. I cannot tell you all I have in mind, but this much I will say. Three different times I have had a certain dream. Each time a sacred person talks about our village and tells me that our troubles will not be solved by ourselves alone, that we must go outside of ourselves to find help. I don't know yet what this means. But meantime we must prepare. Someone may have to make a journey, and at my age that is out of the question. If a journey must be attempted, it will have to fall on a young man; one who thinks of his people, not of himself; one who will give his life, if necessary, in order to save his people."

"This I would do if you asked me. When will you name the first task?"

For some time Salt had sat facing the Holy One. Now he saw the tight skin pucker around the eyes and he heard the old man's cackling laugh.

"You are so anxious to be away, you hardly hear what I am telling you. I tell you again, you are starting something which may end with your giving your life."

"Better that than fall down the cliff and break my neck.

If I give my life helping the people, I cannot give it stupidly. I am listening, Grandfather."

"Good. Now, let me tell you. I want to know how good your wits really are. If you were in a strange country and had to find your way where no way was known to you, or lose your life, how would you succeed? That is your first task."

The words puzzled Salt. "I don't understand."

"Patience, clansman. I haven't explained yet. Look, the Village of the White Rocks was built a long time ago. It already existed when my grandfather was born. Before it was built, according to the story he told, our people lived to the south and west of here. Their houses were small, families were scattered, and they lived in a broad valley where abundant waters flowed, and their corn and bean patches stretched all across that valley. I can believe how happy those people were, with their storage houses always full and never a poor growing season. Then a terrible thing happened. Without warning, Sun Father, whether it was in wrath that people who enjoyed abundance should somehow fail in their duties to him, no one knew, but he threw a great flaming mountain at our people. When it struck, a powerful explosion occurred and burning rock flowed into the fields, and even dried up some of the streams. The people threw down whatever they held in their hands and fled. Mothers even threw down their babies, but afterward went back to find them—and sometimes the babies were not there—nothing was there but smoke and devastation."

"That is why our Sun Crier speaks of the world that died in fire!" The words burst from Salt, heedlessly interrupting the ancient speaker.

"You are correct, but you interrupt."

"I ask to be forgiven."

"It is forgotten. Our people left that broad, pleasant valley and journeyed a long time, seeking safety and new places to plant their crops. They came to the mountains and moved up into many sheltering canyons. Not only the people of our village, but many others had lived in the open valley where the mountain of fire struck the earth. They say that for a long time those people kept moving into the mountains, and into the canyons where they could feel safe from Sun Father. They went into caves, like our own great cave of the White Rocks. There they felt secure, since He Who Rides the Sky could observe their houses for only a few hours of each day."

The Holy One paused when he came to that point. Another thought came upon him and diverted his story.

"Maybe they were foolish—but remember, they were frightened."

"I say nothing against our grandfathers," Salt announced solemnly. He missed the sudden sparkle in the old eyes watching him. "It is not proper for me to speak against the ancient ones. But in our time, much foolishness is talked, and our people live in dark holes like animals. Grandfather, I love the Sun, our Father Sun, and I believe we should no longer dwell in caves."

Salt glanced up, and his face felt suddenly hot when he saw how the Holy One smiled at him.

"Perhaps you will be the one to lead them away from here. Perhaps you will return our people to the broad valley and the gleaming waters."

"I don't know about that, but I would like to lead them down below, where their cornfields would receive the water from our spring."

The smile passed from the old man's face and his voice deepened. "Our corn crop suffers from something more than the want of water. I cannot talk of that now. Another time. Only I must tell you that by planting where you did, you offended the feelings of many. But worse, you gave somebody who moves against us in the dark a chance to blame you for the disaster which may be planned. Thus would you be destroyed, and with you our leadership as Turquoise men."

The words were spoken softly, almost in kindness, but each struck Salt with the force of a blow from a man's hand and set his ears to ringing. Never had he been so sternly rebuked.

Weakly he encountered: "I was a child, I see. You have said our people live in darkness, and I thought I would find the light for them to follow."

The old man tossed the matted gray hair back from his eyes, and was smiling once more.

"True, I have told you that our people live in darkness. An old man may talk thus if, in addition to his years, he has listened to many, has reflected on what was said, and maybe learned something of the purpose of life. It is not a rebuke, but I remind you to expect faults in others and to bend your words to travel around their faults.

"But now we have got ourselves on a strange trail and have to go back. Your task—that is what I must talk about."

"Yes, Grandfather."

"When our people moved into the cave of the White Rocks and built the village, they made a secret trail from the village to the flat land above. It was thought that, if ever disaster should come, the people should have a secret way of escape. Only three living men know about the trail, where it starts and where it ends. When one of the three is about to die, he passes his knowledge on to his successor. If more people knew of it, an enemy might come to know, and we could be destroyed.

"My clansman, you are to find this secret road—and when you find it you are to tell no one. I will have to warn you also that if two of the three discover what you are trying to do, they may destroy you. I, the third one, will be your only protection if you are discovered, but they may act without asking who sent you, and I cannot tell them beforehand that I intend you to be my successor."

Now he looked at the boy. "That is your task. Are you afraid?"

Salt sat speechless, feeling his heart pump loudly—for a moment he actually heard it in his ears.

"This is a heavy task, Grandfather." In his mind, he thought that he must not be rash; he must consider carefully before he spoke.

"One more warning, clansman." The man's voice turned suddenly harsh and cold. "If you decide you cannot or will not try it, I will have to put my flint knife to your

throat with my own hand. No one can know there is a
secret trail from our village unless he is one of the three.
If you know that such a thing exists, you must become one
of us. You cannot know about it and remain apart from us.
So what is your choice?"

It seemed to Salt that a wind out of the dead of winter
swept up his back and brushed the hair at his neck.

"I will find this road, Grandfather. And I will live to
come back and tell you of it."

Chapter 6

Friend and Foe Together

WHEN Salt reached the middle street running through the cliff village he walked swiftly, silently. He was relieved to find the street empty. It seemed quite possible that he could reach his mother's house and climb the ladder without being observed. He need only tread lightly, hold his breath, and presently he would be out of sight. He looked ahead, measuring the short distance still to cover.

He had just passed a jutting wall, when he heard suppressed laughter, the sound he had dreaded. Good sense told him that he should not turn to look, but he turned, nevertheless, and saw the same young girls who had blocked his path the day before. In one voice they sang out: "Did you lose your pretty badge? Did you lose your pretty badge?"

And the voice of the older girl rose up above the others: "Hush, children! Our uncle is trying to find out where the men are meeting. They forgot to tell him!"

The laughter rang out clear and shrill. Salt desired above all else to run the last few steps, but he held to his stride. A moment later he was at the foot of the ladder that would rescue him from shame.

In reality, his progress through the street had been observed from within the shadows of many house openings and from roof tops as well. The seemingly deserted village was alive that morning with gossip and rumor. People might stand out of the boy's way, as they would turn their gaze away from any person who would be embarrassed by their watching, but they were not any less curious about the things that were being told. It was a courtesy not to pry openly into another's affairs.

One who watched from a shadowed doorway was Flute Man, his mind still aflame from the indignities heaped upon him since the previous day. He would be on the watch henceforth, until his hand performed the deed which his wits had not shifted to another.

Another watcher was Star Climber, Salt's age mate, who had been thunderstruck when he was told the purpose of the kiva meeting. His hands trembled and he felt a tightening in his chest, as if he expected a similar blow to fall upon him.

When the words of the Sun Crier had died away, Star Climber heard himself muttering: "They will turn him into a child again. Surely he has done some terrible thing. Never have I heard of this before. What may happen to me, for have I not been his friend since we were children together? But if they ask me, I shall say I know nothing, and whatever it is, I don't approve. I cannot be blamed."

Star Climber was so slow of understanding and so timid at the same time, it was just as well he stayed out of sight and made no effort to catch up with his hurrying friend. Salt was not in a mood to explain what was to happen.

An air of foreboding and a reluctance to proceed lay heavily upon that meeting. Each man as he descended the ladder felt that some decision would be required of him, and each felt that someone else should be responsible. This reluctance even reached to the four principal officers, who sat near the weak fire in the center of the room and passed the short-stemmed pipe from hand to hand. When one pipe had been smoked cold, a second pipe was prepared and sent around. Then, instead of opening the meeting, the one having the title of Fire Tender or Fire Chief was directed to bring cedar bark for the fire, and as the pungent smoke arose it was aspersed to the four directions by the Sun Watcher. Still no one spoke.

The only one in the room who wished the meeting to proceed was Flute Man. He sat restlessly while the kiva officers prolonged their smoking. A number of times he straightened his shoulders, as if preparing himself to speak. Then he would look at his near neighbors on either side, perhaps to encourage them to call for action. But it was a reluctant meeting.

The boy, Star Climber, had found a spot in the deepest shadow. He was wishing that no one would even notice his presence in the room. He kept his eyes to the ground immediately in front of his folded legs.

Finally, the four officers arose from their places around the fire pit and moved to their appointed seats. Trailing Cloud, who had the title of Sun Watcher and was the senior officer of the kiva, indicated that he would speak. He coughed, then he sighed. "If anyone is to speak, let him start now." He sighed once more and relaxed.

The rule of procedure required a formal statement of the business to come before the meeting, a statement usually given by the leader of the society concerned. In a question involving hunting, the War Chief spoke first. In this case, Cloud Head, the chief of the Masked God society which conducted the initiation ceremonies, was responsible. But Cloud Head, like the others, did not want to start.

Flute Man fidgeted. Staring at Cloud Head, he all but called upon him to begin.

Finally, Cloud Head rose; a short, stout man, with a surprisingly powerful voice. His black hair was cropped in jagged edges and bound by a band of twisted material.

"I did not call this meeting," he announced in a voice that battered the walls. "But you know what was announced at sunrise. Eldest Woman sent word to deal with this boy. Someone else may know the reason for this. I do not. If you want it done, I will carry out your wishes. That is all I have to say at this time."

When Cloud Head returned to his seat, breathing loudly, the room was silent again. A man coughed, another scratched loudly.

Trailing Cloud looked up in surprise. He had expected the meeting to start, but instead it was back in his hands. He was fretful in his old age, and the fact that he had to be helped to his feet irritated him. Surely so much trouble was unnecessary.

"Someone will have to speak," he said sharply. He was too shortsighted to recognize faces at arm's length away, but he squinted around him as if he could see plainly. "You know it is not my place to begin. We have been called together, now it is for you to explain why we are here. Start the meeting!" He did not sit down at once but continued to squint into vacancy.

Flute Man arose. It was still not his turn, but he wanted something to happen. The others might hesitate to act because they did not want to shame that boy, or because they were in the dark. But he knew what he wanted. Let them get started!

When the squinting Sun Watcher failed to see him in the dim room, Flute Man spoke out: "I am ready, Grandfather. This boy of whom we speak is my sister's child. I know about this matter."

Trailing Cloud not only ignored him but turned his face in the other direction.

"I know the speaker, Flute Man, and I don't want to hear him. Let someone else speak at this time."

Flute Man was shocked by the harshness of the old man's rebuff. It was the first hint that the meeting might go against him. These men would not bend to him, as he intended they should, unless he could stand straight before them and speak with the weight of his office. They must remember that the War Chief could retaliate.

The exchange of words started a murmuring, a general stirring and shifting of bodies, as if the men had become aware of tension. Cloud Head stood up, frowning, seeming to suggest that he had been ready all the time.

"This is not my wish," he boomed. "Our young clansman, the boy we call Salt, is accused of acting in some manner, I don't know what, to bring shame upon himself and upon us, his elder brothers. We are asked to put him out of the kiva and turn him back to the children. This has never been done in my lifetime, though I know it was done in other times. We have a way of doing it. Our Masked God society must be called together for the initiation ceremony, only we will perform it backward. This will take practice, since none of us have done it before. If you want this done, tell us, so we will know. We must take the whip from the boy's back if he is to be put out of the kiva."

"Why do this to one of our brothers?" The question came out of the shadows.

"I tell you all I know," Cloud Head thundered back. "Eldest Woman sent word that it should be done. Indeed, she has already taken away the turquoise badge, so the boy is now without protection."

The Sun Watcher spoke from where he sat. "It is only our protection which is taken away. He is now, like all

children, protected by Sun, our Father. He is safe enough.
If Eldest Woman wishes the wrongway ceremony performed, I think we must do it. She has her reasons for what
she asks. It is something for all of us to decide."

Star Climber, in his shadowed spot, had raised his head.
He began to feel that these men, with their reluctance,
were not bent upon destroying him or his friend, although
he could not fully understand the turns and twists in their
talk. He watched the firelight play upon the faces, his ears
alert to each voice, to anger or treachery. Flute Man had
attacked Salt at other kiva meetings. Did he now speak as
enemy, or as friend?

Flute Man had risen again, and the boy in the shadows
hugged his knees tightly. He thought: Now it will come.
Something terrible will happen, and I am here watching it.

The voice of Flute Man was subdued, as if he had decided to guard his words and his manner. "I ask permission
to speak."

Trailing Cloud, in the place of authority, waved his
assent. "The matter has been stated. You may speak."

"I am grateful. I speak for this boy, whose mother is
my sister. You have heard me speak harshly to him, even
here in this kiva. That was when he deserved rebuke. Now
I speak in his favor, for I am one who knows how to be
fair. It is a shameful thing we talk of doing to this boy.
We are told that Eldest Woman wants this done. Are we
to act blindly and shame our younger brother? We are
men, here, and the decision is with us, as our Sun Watcher
reminds us. I say the boy should have his badge restored
and he should come back to the kiva."

Flute Man glanced here and there, as if to see who would support him. His long thin face seemed to float by itself in the pale light that spread downward from the square opening in the kiva roof.

Silence, then. Until a voice hissed out of the shadows, "A child that walks in the protection of the sun, will not be killed in darkness."

Flute Man jumped forward, trembling. "Who speaks?" he shouted. He would have leaped over the seated forms in front of him, if a hand had not grasped his arm.

"Easy, brother. Here we are having a kiva meeting."

"Someone speaks lies!" Flute Man struggled, but could not loosen the grip.

Star Climber, who had put his hands over his face, glanced through open fingers and saw Flute Man straining. Perhaps there will be a fight, here in the kiva! he thought. The very possibility made him tremble. The kiva was a place for calmness and order; it was the place where one made prayer sticks and honored the supernatural people.

Across the room the voice of Trailing Cloud snapped like a whip. He did not rise, but it was as if he suddenly towered over all.

"Turn that man loose! And you, Flute Man, stand back! There, now. When you ask for permission to speak, and it is granted, you are expected to act properly. You know it without my telling you."

"I am at fault," acknowledged Flute Man, still panting. He saw clearly that he would not have his way. It might even go harder against him.

"Very well. Now, you say a lie has been spoken. What is the lie?"

Flute Man opened his mouth to speak boldly. Then closed it as quickly.

"I couldn't tell who spoke. Someone over there," he jutted chin and lips to indicate the opposite side of the room.

"I did not ask who. I asked what lie was spoken."

"Perhaps I spoke too fast. I did not intend to say that word."

"All right. Then no lie was spoken. Who was it that talked?"

Day Singer rose across the room. In the dull light the red cloth which bound his graying hair looked black. His broad, unsmiling face was a pale moon.

"I was the one who spoke. I wish to ask this man why he wants our young brother brought back to the kiva. I say it is not because he loves him. And I remind every man here that whoever harms a child harms us all, and we will pay it back."

Flute Man looked here and there at the faces around him, wondering what was known, what guessed at, and what hands would be raised against him.

He gestured, as if to brush the matter aside. "I spoke for the sake of the boy. He is my sister's child. I wish him respected."

"Then," Day Singer continued, relentlessly, "you will be content to see his childhood protected. Respect and protect are twins."

"Who says he needs protection?" Flute Man fired back.

"We are all brothers here. If I am accused of something, let me know what it is." People of the village often said they could not understand Flute Man. His voice was hard when there seemed to be no need of it. He always talked louder than was necessary. When a kiva leader placed him in charge of some small office, even if it was no more than gathering and storing the corn from the clan lands, he issued orders, as if the entire village were under his command.

Day Singer stood staring. He started to reply, then checked himself. He turned to the officers in the center of the room. "I have decided that Shield should answer this man. I have a rude tongue and I may say something to harm us all. Shield, my uncle in the clan, knows what is in my mind. He will answer as he sees fit."

"Shield can answer, if he desires," Trailing Cloud said in a tone that indicated clearly that he did not care. "For myself, I think the man needs no answer. He questions our wisdom for wanting to protect the boy. Let it rest there."

"I will answer for our wisdom," Shield replied, rising tall among them. The bones in his face made shadows in the half-light, as did the wells of his eyes. Seen with these shadows upon it, it was a face of thoughtfulness and hidden purposes.

"We accuse no man here," the quiet voice said. Shield stood not far from Flute Man, regarding him. "It is of the boy, Salt, we are thinking. He will be a leader among us someday; only now he is impatient and wants to be a leader at once, before he has grown into it. We think it best that he have a little time to think about the duties of a leader. Our clansman here, Flute Man, knows that we are not looking for harm to come to the boy. The sun will truly watch his movements, and if the sun fails, which is unthinkable, there will be eyes to watch. Our clansman knows this."

When Shield withdrew to his stone bench against the wall, there was murmured approval. Tension seemed to go out of the room. Flute Man had been warned, but so skilfully that it was as the shadow of a bird passing out of sight. He must know how the kiva felt about this, yet nothing had been said to offend him. He could withdraw decently. Shield was a clever man in such matters. The murmuring went all around the room.

Star Climber, in his corner, breathed freely at last. His hands no longer covered his face and he felt happy to be present at a meeting where everything was turning out so well.

Trailing Cloud put his approval on Shield's words by declaring the meeting at an end. But first, he gave instructions: "We will proceed with the wrongway ceremony. Cloud Head will instruct his people in the Masked God society. In four days, we will return, and the boy, Salt, will be brought in. The whip will be taken from his back."

The men responded with their calls of "Good! Good!"

Flute Man was at the ladder. Then he was gone. Only he knew how frightened he had been toward the end. Frightened at the thought that someone in the kiva knew of the owl's claw tucked away under his belt. Day Singer might be the one, or even Shield, in all his mildness.

Fear still went with him into the open air, like a thong looped around his middle and biting the flesh. If his Turquoise clansmen were truly against him and waited only for the time when they might destroy him, then he must know and join openly with Dark Dealer and the Spider Clan. But he would not do that until the last moment, when he knew certainly that he could not retreat. For there was no safety in Dark Dealer.

Chapter 7

Beware of Owls

IT WAS hard to believe in a secret trail. Salt had been born in a house lying under the cliff and lived all his days scrambling over the rubble of rock, exploring eagles' nests on high crags, hunting rabbits in the flat land above the cliff. He knew the trail that led from the village to the bottom of the canyon and also the trail that twisted and climbed to the upper country. No secret about these, since the people of the village used them every day. It wasn't that he doubted the word of the Holy One, but it was like being told that summer comes twice in a year or that he could enter his own house without going through the opening in the roof.

After leaving the cave house of the Holy One that morning, he spent the entire day alone, stopping at home only long enough to put two handfuls of parched corn in the buckskin bag he carried at his waist. He would find the secret trail, as he had promised, though he would start with a heavy heart. He fled to the flat country above the canyon to begin the search, but most of all to be by himself.

For he was troubled. In the course of one day's journey of the sun, he had himself traveled from a boy's concern with the hunting of rabbits to a knowledge of the dangers with which his elders lived. It was a long journey to make in so short a time. His mind had to take it in. His flesh had to find warmth again. He had to learn how to act in a threatening world.

The elders were fond of saying that, if a man expected to find truth, he should seek it alone. Salt was not sure it meant the same thing, but he had discovered that he could think better, and indeed he often felt better, when he went off by himself. On some of his lonely excursions, he thought only of going as far and as fast as he could, and he would run and walk by turns, until at day's end he had passed beyond his known world. Then, if he had killed a rabbit with his throwing stick or snared a bird in his net of woven hair, he would kindle a fire and eat. Or if his running and walking left him too exhausted to hunt, he fed meagerly on parched corn and crawled among warm rocks to sleep. His mother never fretted over these absences; she knew that they were a part of his growing time.

On other excursions, he delighted himself just in looking at things. He might sit on a rock while the sun moved
all the way across the sky and watch the comings and goings
of a colony of ants. He would shred the tip of a sliver of
yucca to make a fine brush, and with a quick paint of
saliva and white clay, he would daub the backs of some
ants to tell them apart. Then he would smile to himself
as he began to understand which ones went out to forage
for food, which others labored at hauling grains of sand
out of the underground house, and which appeared to act
as guards or warriors of the house. It was a fine thing, he
thought, just to watch an ant making a world for itself.
That was almost as good as running to cover distance and
get away from human talk.

That day when Salt went to the flat country above the
cliffs, it was to look again at a land that he knew well. The
people called it the flat country, but really it was not flat.
The earth rose in round hills, with shallow valleys between,
or it lay in long ridges out of which an edge of broken
brown rocks showed like the teeth of a monster. The low-
growing pinon and cedar trees which, close at hand, appeared so green, turned blue-black in the distance. Knife-
leafed yucca plants and cholla cactus grew between the
trees. The women prized the yucca, because from its roots
they made a fine froth in which they washed their hair.
In other clear spaces the grass grew thick and made moving
patterns in the wind, and the grass was prized by the deer
and antelope, whose flashing tails might be seen through
the pine trees on almost any day one came up from the
canyon.

One breathed freer in this open country. One's fears and doubts, if they were the fears and doubts of a boy growing up, fell away, and one's heart grew light again.

Up here in the flat country were the planted fields from which the Village of the White Rocks drew life and the songs that fill a life. These fields stretched from almost the rim of the canyon to the very point at which the sky came down to the land. Along this entire reach, the earth was quite level, except that it sloped from each side toward the center, as if it had been the bowl of an old lake. The field that belonged to Salt's family was about midway along and toward the low center. Each family placed a boundary of sticks and stones around its plot. Each of the Seven Clans making up the village had its own land, and these lands, too, were marked off and a boundary post gave the sign for the clan.

The fields were never deserted. Even when the cleaning out of weeds had been completed and the plants had only to grow and fulfil themselves, men from the village remained close by. They might be out of sight in a clump of cedar trees, but they were there, watching. Deer liked the tender top growth of corn; ground squirrels were fond of succulent roots; crows waited for the ears to fill. Many walking and crawling animals besides the people of the village waited to feast on the corn, beans, and squash that grew in those fields. An even greater danger, one that folk preferred not to mention, were the hungry peoples who came down from the north, sometimes from the east, and carried off entire crops. They too waited until the ripening time, and when they came, the flat country was filled with fierce shouting and moans and the sound of clubs and stones striking dully on flesh.

Today, Salt was mindful of the men watching from the trees. He must be careful not to appear to be looking for anything, or they would come and offer to join in the search. He knew how tiresome it became sitting through the day with nothing to do but watch clouds and learn new songs from an elder uncle, and he decided it would be better to act the part of a child at play, wandering aimlessly in the sun. It would be reported in the kiva, of course, that he was not performing his duties as he should, and not helping his family. That could not be helped.

In considering the secret trail, he had decided that it was impossible to look for it in the village. It might start from one of the seven kivas, or even from under the floor of a house. Prying into such places was unlikely to accomplish results. But since the trail was planned as an escape to the country above the cliffs, it could be assumed that somewhere up here he would find the other end. That is, if the trail really existed.

He worked out a game of playing eagle; at least anyone watching him from the trees would guess it was that. To play the game, he would find a mound of rocks or a low hill. There he would stand poised, appearing to survey the land stretched out below his perch. He would move his head from side to side. Then, with outstretched arms, he would swoop down from his high place and run, not too fast, in long sweeping curves that took him through pine thickets and open spaces, and he would tilt his arms as he

turned and peered at the ground. When he pounced for
the kill, he would leap high and come down on all fours.
That allowed him time to search the mound of earth
around a badger hole or to scratch away the brown needles
at the base of a pine tree. He hardly knew what he was
looking for, but somewhere, if his eyes were sharp, he
would find a sign, a stray footprint, a worn place in the
grass, a marking on a rock, something that would lead him
to his goal.

As he played his game into the afternoon, with one part
of his mind always aware of the men and boys who might
be watching from the planted fields, Salt forgot about two
others who might also be watching.

The Holy One had said that the secret of the hidden
trail was known to three, of which he was himself one.
That was all he said, except to warn Salt that he would go
in peril when he tried to find the trail.

And thus it happened, on that first day of Salt's searching, that two watched from a hiding place which gave them
a view over the entire sweep of land. They watched, and
were puzzled.

One of these, Day Singer, was especially concerned. He
was stocky and powerful, though his hair was beginning
to gray and deep erosions crossed his brow. His headband
of red woven stuff marked him as one of the speakers in
the kiva. His manners were blunt, yet he was known in
his family for his gentleness with children. The women
complained that he spoiled the children, would not make

them mind; but possibly that was because the children
flocked to him when he entered a house and became deaf
to their mothers.

His companion was Turtle, of the Water-Reed Clan—
sometimes called the Younger Sister Clan, since the legend
told that these people followed closely behind the Turquoise clansmen in their trip from the south. Turtle was
older, thin and tall; talkative and complaining. He found
fault with his relatives, his health, the conduct of kiva
officials, the lack of rain, and the failure of the young
people to listen when their elders spoke. He carried always
a long staff, which he claimed his aging legs required, but
the young men jeered that he used the staff for probing
and prying. He too bound his hair with a band of woven
cotton, its color a turquoise blue.

Looking out from the hiding place where they sat side
by side, Day Singer expressed his concern: "What is that
boy doing up here? I have already protected him in the
kiva—what must I do now?"

He continued to watch and to frown.

Turtle added his own grumbling: "He is too big a boy
for playing that kind of nonsense. What is he up to? He
runs back and forth like a dog searching for something."

The boy was not too far away, and it almost seemed as
if he were following some design which brought him closer
and closer. Day Singer moved restlessly.

"If he should find this trail—" Turtle asked, but felt
too uncomfortable to finish his question.

"Our duty is to destroy him," Day Singer replied,
unhappy.

"But he is your kinsman. If he comes, I will take care of him."

"No. We are both responsible. My hand will be against him too."

They pursued the matter no further, for at that moment their attention was drawn to a second figure moving in the country below them.

Salt had been playing his game for several hours when an owl called out, faintly, as if from a great distance.

No one liked to hear owl talk. It was bad enough at night, though that was the normal time for the creatures to converse among themselves. But an owl in the daytime could only mean danger, bad luck, or someone passing into death.

Owls were the spirits of the dead. Since they were not human, not limited by human weaknesses, they could perform alarming feats of strength and magic. Every household had owl stories—a certain man was lured to his death over a cliff; another man rolled dice for his own head, and lost; a woman followed an owl, crying like a child, and was lost in a blizzard. Children, listening, never forgot such stories.

One story was told of a handsome young man who was crushed to death by a stone rolling from a mountain ledge just as he was on his way to the house of the beautiful girl he was to marry. Immediately after that unhappy event, a snow-white owl appeared in a tall hemlock tree that rose from the canyon bottom. For several nights the villagers saw and heard the great white bird. It talked in low mourn-

ing tones. On the fourth day, just as dusk gathered in the
cliff village, the large white creature sailed on spread wings
into the village itself, plucked the girl from a gathering
of people who were too frightened even to utter a sound,
beat its wings rapidly until it was clear of the cliff walls,
and sailed to a pinnacle of rock that stood by itself far
down the canyon. The walls of this pinnacle were so sheer
and high that no man could climb it. For days afterward,
the people in the village could hear the girl crying to be
rescued, but none could reach her, though many tried.
Finally, they heard her no more, nor did they ever see
the white owl again.

The cry of an owl in midafternoon was certainly a bad
thing. As soon as Salt heard it, he stopped his game. It was
as if a black cloud had come swiftly up the sky to blot out
the sun. The suddenness of it left him in breathless confusion.

He stood rigid for several moments, as his thoughts
darted about. An instinct told him to run, but he seemed
to know that if he ran, his fear would increase, until he
would be running away from the thought of being afraid.
While he stood swaying between the impulse to run and
the impulse to stand his ground, he looked into the near
trees, but saw nothing. Then with great effort of mind, he
turned around, moved a few feet and looked in the direction of the ridge of broken rocks.

He expected to see nothing. No bird. No movement
among the treetops or in the knee-high grass. No sound.
Small desert birds which had been chirping, stopped, as if
they were watching something. A hunter following game

knew the sensation. Salt remembered just in time. Or maybe it was the single snapping sound behind him.

He leaped sharply to his right. An arrow whistled past his head and drove itself into the ground a few feet beyond where he had been standing. He heard the muffled crack of the flint head as it struck a buried stone.

In one forward motion, he grabbed the arrow, snapping the shaft at the point where it entered the hard ground, and ran.

As he ran, he realized that he was not frightened. He was angry, but not frightened or confused. He was running from a living man, an armed enemy, who might be notching another arrow. That was something one knew and understood. Not an owl talking of death, but a prowling hunter.

Salt ran on, as swift and sure-footed as the deer that flashed through the woods. And as he ran he examined the feathered shaft in his hand and recognized the workmanship. No man could disguise his own handiwork.

Chapter 8

Conversation at Dawn

THE WOMAN called The Eldest had a longer, more formal name, which the people of the village rarely used; many perhaps had forgotten that she was The-Woman-Who-Rises-to-the-Top-of-Dawn-Mountain. The name Eldest Woman was actually a title, borne in each generation by the oldest woman in the direct line of descent from the legendary founder of the clan; she need not be the oldest woman in age within the clan; in fact, The-Woman-Who-Rises had been called Eldest Woman ever since she was a young married woman, and everyone knew her in that way.

82

Although advanced in years and short of breath, she still arose in the early dawn and started her day of toil. Upon arising, she ran a brush of shredded yucca fibers through her thinning gray hair. Then she picked up the little bag of corn pollen from its place in a wall niche and anointed first her forehead, then her lips, and finally a few grains of the powdery substance were allowed to fall upon the pallet upon which she had lain. Thus, with her head blessed for clear thoughts, her lips reminded to speak truthfully, and her bed commended for having given rest, she hunched herself together and squeezed through the narrow opening which led to the roof terrace outside her topmost room. Her house, which was the tallest in the village, reached almost to the overlying rock, and at dawn it was still black night under the roof of the cave.

Age had not destroyed her sense of balance. When she came to the ladder projecting up from the terrace below, she threw her short leg over the parapet and walked down without touching her hands to the ladder.

A figure shrouded in darkness moved on this lower terrace. Coals glowed red for a moment, subsided, then glowed again. A breath was bringing them to life. A tiny flame spurted.

"May you have happiness in this new day, young one," Eldest Woman greeted the fire maker.

A young woman's face was dimly lighted by the pale fire. "You move like a star, Grandmother. I heard nothing. May all days bring peace to you," came the reply.

"I go below, but will return soon."

"The heated pot and I will be waiting."

When she had descended two more ladders, walking erect and facing forward, Eldest Woman emerged in a kind of courtyard. Walls surrounded the small square, where people waited. The darkness was so intense that the waiting ones were sensed rather than seen; anyway, they were expected. As soon as Eldest Woman touched her feet to the stone pavement, voices uttered greetings of the morning. Bodies moved about. The odor of smoke, clinging to hair and clothing, identified the shadows as women. Their cooking fires were with them, even when they were not laboring at their pots.

"Are we all here? Are more to come?" Eldest Woman tried to make out the number of forms around her.

"I think we have one more than usual—I can't rightly tell," a voice explained.

"So? Is there a new one present? Speak up. All are welcome."

"I came, not for food, Mother, but to speak with you."

Eldest Woman moved forward, raising a hand to avoid colliding with anyone who might stand in the way.

"Who is it, then, my Daughter?"

Then her hands cupped themselves around the form of a face. She knew finally who it was.

"Ah, yes. Indeed. We will talk. Just wait."

She moved across the enclosure and squeezed herself through an entrance as narrow as the one from her sleeping room. House doors were built with a high sill that helped to check cold air from creeping in at the floor level, and their narrowness also made it easier to keep out an unwelcome intruder. In really cold weather a hanging of thick cotton cloth or a fur robe was placed over the opening.

"Now, my daughters, bring your jars, or whatever you have. Here is corn, dried squash, beans, and dried meat for your babes and your ailing ones. Bring a jar here, where my hand is reaching. Our storeroom may not be bottomless, but for our mothers who are without men and our children who are without elders, we always have enough. Bring your jars or your baskets. You belong to the House of Turquoise, and there is abundance among us."

Eldest Woman continued to chatter as she filled jars and baskets. Each woman, upon receiving a brimming measure in her receptacle, murmured a blessing and hurried away. In the darkness of the early dawn, none might see who came to the clan storehouse to receive a gift of food. No one ever spoke of such things. The names of the women, or the children, who appeared at the storehouse were never uttered in the hearing of others.

They had gone at last, except one who waited by the ladder descending into the courtyard. Eldest Woman squeezed her way through the storehouse doorway and moved toward the waiting figure.

"Now, mother of the boy Salt, you wish to talk and I am ready to listen. It is as well that we stay where we are, since we will not be interrupted."

Salt's mother, Becoming Day, was small and slender. She made only a slight shadow at the foot of the ladder. The hands that moved so swift and true in pottery making held firm to a mantle of woven cotton that covered her head and was gathered under her chin. Her upturned eyes caught a glint from an early morning fire and seemed like dark wells of questioning.

"How will it end, my Mother? I have a heaviness in my heart that I speak to no one about, only to you. How will it end? At tomorrow's sunrise the men in the kiva will begin the ceremony which returns my son to childhood. Perhaps a mother should rejoice to have a child restored— but I cannot rejoice. They tell me this is a protection for him—that no one will harm him. Yet, two days ago, as he walked on the land above, someone shot an arrow that would have pierced him through the back, if he had not leaped aside. And yesterday, as he followed the trail which leads from our village to the land above, a stone gave way under his foot. If he had not made a strong leap, he would have been dashed to the bottom. How is he being protected, I ask myself, when these things occur?"

The soft, hurried voice caught for a moment, as if the dark eyes were staring into a chasm and watching a boulder, which might have been her son, strike on stone, and fly far out into space.

Eldest Woman stood silently, waiting. She knew the other woman must talk, so she waited with bowed head.

"He had not strayed from the path, he tells me. It was a stone right there before him, one on which he had trod many times. I knew the place well when he described it. It is a stone we have all trod on. Somehow it had been loosened, and was waiting for him.

"What will happen before another sun sets? What will happen after they hold this wrongway ceremony? He will be a child and will go unarmed. How will he defend himself against this enemy who shoots from ambush and lays traps for him? How will it end? That is what lies in my heart."

Eldest Woman reached across to touch the cheek of the other woman. That was the only mark of tenderness she displayed and it was more than usual.

"I cannot answer these questions. They must lie with you, must twist your heart, until they are answered."

Daylight was now seeping in under the cliff, bringing the forms of houses out of darkness. The two women standing so close together could each see the troubled face of the other. Each knew that talk would solve nothing, yet talk was still a comfort.

"Men are moving, here and there, out of our sight," Eldest Woman continued. "They move against all of us, not against your boy alone. You say the boy is not protected, because he goes unarmed, as a child should. But why did he leap away from the arrow shot from ambush? Why was he not swept into the canyon with the rock that turned under his foot? I say he is protected by Father Sun. Remember it."

The clan mother moved away, looking carefully for eyes that might be watching from the walls and terraces above; then returned. Her voice dropped to a thin whisper.

"This day, and the night to come, will be decisive. Before another sun rises from his morning bed, some men will stand and some will fall. How it will be, I cannot yet tell. It is not clear. The boy, Salt, will have his part in it.

"Now, we must go. A pair of eyes watches from some-

where. I cannot find them, but they are there. We will
mount the ladder and go to our morning work."

When they had reached the first terrace, Eldest Woman
paused to look again. Then she whispered, her voice so low
that Salt's mother almost imagined rather than heard the
words:

"Your boy will want to go again to the flat country. Do
not stop him, but tell him to watch carefully. Today, the
coyotes will be around. Go now."

She watched Salt's mother cross the terrace and climb
to a set of buildings standing in the opposite direction from
her own tower house. Then she turned to go her way. Her
eyes missed nothing. She saw the quick withdrawal of a
head within a doorway halfway across the village. Today
would be the day, surely.

In the few minutes it took for her to reach her own cooking fire, The-Woman-Who-Rises-to-the-Top-of-Dawn-
Mountain remembered many things out of her life. Some
of them she remembered with sorrow. They came into
mind without bidding because, in some way unknown to
herself, she had a feeling, or an insight, of what was to
come. This would be a day when the good that was in men
would prove itself or be destroyed. And in such a day were
the seeds of future sorrows.

It brought a moment of pain still, after almost fifty
years, to recall the loss of her son child. She had been
gathering pinon nuts up in the flat country and had left
her first-born on a blanket of woven rabbit fur. She was a
short distance away, reaching with a long pole to dislodge
the fat cones. At first she had the impression of a cloud

passing over the sun—after all these years, when the sun disappeared under a fast-moving cloud, she felt a sudden fright. On that day, the shadow swept over her, then she heard rather than saw the beating of heavy wings. They made a rumbling in the air. She rushed from behind the spreading limbs of the pinon tree, just in time to see a golden eagle of massive wingspread rise into flight. Its talons were securely locked in the flesh of the infant. She heard no outcry.

In her effort to erase the pain, her mind rushed on, into a scene of later anguish.

In the Village of the White Rocks, brother and sister relations were always close, but Eldest Woman and her brother were especially so, since both parents had perished in a snowstorm and left them in the care of aged grand-parents whose household was made up of a great crowd of quarrelsome children and grandchildren. Through the shoutings and rivalries of many years, the orphaned pair protected and supported each other. When Eldest Woman married, she returned to her mother's house, as was proper; and her brother, on his marriage, went to the house of his wife's kin. That, too, was proper. He gathered the load of wood for his wife's mother which made him as one with the new household. As the years passed, brother and sister saw little of each other, though actually no day went by without one hearing news of the other.

After many years the brother, because he was trusted, as his family had been trusted before him, and be-cause he was a man of peace, rose to be Village Chief. His name was then Blue Evening Sky, a good name, since blue was the color of the west and the color, as well, of peace and serenity. In a word, it was the color of turquoise.

He served the people and observed the duties of his office with great care. It was not an easy load to carry. The Village Chief was, in a way, a prisoner of his people. He might never leave the village, because if he did the crops might fail, springs might run dry, and people might perish of hunger and thirst. So faithfully did Blue Evening Sky observe this rule, that he rarely went even to the limits of the village, but on any day could be found either in his house, in the kiva, or in the plaza, which was in fact the roof of the kiva. When he sat in the plaza, it was a signal for people to come to him for help or advice.

Above everything, the Village Chief must persuade the people to accept peaceful ways of settling differences. He was not free to go to war, or even to hunt. A hunter always ran the risk of offending the animal world, members of which could retaliate by causing sickness among men, or failure of crops. The chief of the village could not take such a risk. Meat for his table was procured by others, and others also brought wood for his household and planted his crops. Thus, he was free to devote his entire time to the needs of the people. He could keep his thoughts moving toward the ways of peace.

After Blue Evening Sky became chief the years passed quietly; neither hunger nor war interrupted the flow of days. Babes born in the first year of his leadership grew up, married, and started families of their own, and in all that time nothing occurred to trouble the village.

Eldest Woman remembered these years in the minutes

of climbing from the courtyard where she gave out corn and beans to the waiting women. In all that span of years, her brother had kept the people together, kept them free of disastrous quarrels, and they prospered.

She paused at the top of the ladder and tried, as she had many times before, to understand what happened next. Her gaze swept over the tops of buildings into the void that lay beyond, but her eyes were not searching out any object. It was the mind that groped. What had happened? Perhaps—she had thought many times—men are not made for peace. They are animals that must fight among themselves when they have no enemies to contend against. Give them a full meal, and still they hunger for another's food.

Standing at the top of the ladder, she shuddered, trying to shake off troubled thoughts as a dog will shake off water.

It was difficult, indeed, to understand why the men of the Spider Clan, led by Dark Dealer, their new War Chief, came in a body to Blue Evening Sky and demanded that he retire as Chief of the Village of the White Rocks.

Dark Dealer was the spokesman, and a brazen one. He accosted Blue Evening Sky in the little plaza, and stood spread-legged, his men arrayed behind him. They at least observed the courtesy of lowering their eyes.

"We have come to say that we of the Spider Clan can no longer accept your leadership."

That was what Dark Dealer shouted, and what Eldest Woman, years later, still labored to understand. How could a man move so far beyond good manners and still be as one of them?

"You men of the Turquoise Clan have made the people

believe that you were the first to come, and therefore
have the right to decide all matters concerning the village. My clansmen are tired of believing that. Our legends
state that we are an older people, the oldest in the world.
It was Spider who carried the first earth up from the sea
and made the world. So why should we step aside? We
have as much right as the Turquoise people to rule the
village. We think you should share the leadership with
us—let us be the head for a while."

Up to that point, Dark Dealer had talked with loud
arrogance. It was clear that he wanted as many people as
possible to overhear him and to be struck by his fearless-
ness. Never before had anyone addressed the Village Chief
in such a manner. Blue Evening Sky was seated all that
time. He wore a sleeveless tunic of pale-blue cloth, a rope
of many strands of tiny pink shells around his neck,
earrings of sparkling shell, and a dark-blue twisted band
around his bristling gray hair. His manner was calm, and
a smile even played on his lips.

Dark Dealer shifted his feet, he bent his head down
toward the seated leader. He whispered, but the whisper
could be heard beyond the tiny plaza, so quiet was the
waiting crowd.

"Last night one of our strongest men died of an agony
in his belly. Only yesterday he was among us, a powerful
man. Why did he die? My people believe he was bewitched. I am prepared to tell them that a man of the
Turquoise Clan is the witch."

Dark Dealer pulled back, and for the first time smiled.
"Now, what do you say? Will you agree to let a Spider

Clan man succeed you as Village Chief, or shall we come among you and look for our witch?"

It was long afterward that Blue Evening Sky told all this to his sister. He told how at first he could not believe his ears. How he sat and stared at the arrogant speaker, expecting him to remember his manners and go away. He had heard about Dark Dealer, had even seen him around the village, but could not recall ever talking to him.

"When he continued that way," Blue Evening Sky explained, "I could feel something die within me. My lifetime, all I had done to teach peaceful living to our people, died, piece by piece, while that man talked."

When no answer came, Dark Dealer looked annoyed. He shouted: "Well? What have you to say?"

Blue Evening Sky was not a tall man, but neither was Dark Dealer, and when the Village Chief rose to his feet, his face was on a level with his adversary.

The Chief uttered not a word. He stood staring into the eyes that were on a level with his own. Then he spat straight into the arrogant face.

Still without speaking, he resumed his seat.

By that time the plaza had filled with Turquoise men, attracted by the loud voice. Quickly they saw what was happening and moved to cut off Dark Dealer from his bodyguard. Dark Dealer had not noticed that he was now alone, and when he advanced upon the Chief, shouting, "Now, you have done it! Now, you will pay! This is the end of your accursed clan!" he was quickly surrounded. Not a hand touched him, yet he was all but lifted off his feet and rushed from the plaza.

That was how it started. The web of quiet days was torn apart and nothing could put it back. Before long, a Turquoise man was found at dawn with an arrow through his heart. He lay in the center of the plaza, where Dark Dealer had shouted at Blue Evening Sky. Owl feathers were tied to the protruding shaft of the arrow, which meant that the dead man was accused by his killer of witchcraft.

The Village Chief aged swiftly. He tried to keep his own men from committing crimes in retaliation, but he found his strength not equal to it. A Spider clansman was caught alone and hurled over the cliff.

To his sister, Blue Evening Sky lamented: "I am at fault. Through all these years I talked against anger and bad thoughts. I told others to be peaceful. Yet now, when I had a chance to show my people how a man can put aside anger and bad thoughts, just see what I do! An untaught babe could not have done worse!"

He would not be consoled. Indeed, after a while he would not even discuss the matter. When men came to report later acts of bad faith or evildoing, he would babble back at them until they were bewildered.

Before another year had passed, he moved out of the village, to the rock shelter high up in the face of the cliff. He meant it as an act of abdication, but his clansmen, and in fact the villagers as a whole, would not accept the act and still looked to him as leader.

They said: "He is now touched by the powers of the Other World. He is the Holy One, and let no man put a hand on him."

In the Turquoise Clan it was known that the trouble had not ended. Dark Dealer would not let it end. He continued to move against them, and would strike when he was ready.

This was the anguish that Eldest Woman felt in her heart that morning, as she climbed the last ladder and stood finally before her cooking fire.

The face of the young girl was upturned in daylight at last, and she was smiling. "You bring happiness, Grandmother," she murmured.

The searching, searing eyes of the older woman faltered at the words. She looked about, as if on returning from a distant journey she felt surprise at a familiar face and voice.

"You give happiness, child," she said, barely audible.

Chapter 9

Disaster in the Canyon

HAT was the day of the summer solstice—the day on which the sun reached its farthest advance into the northern sky. On that day, and at the winter solstice as well, the village people felt uneasy. Partly, this uneasiness resulted from what they could see with their own eyes: each day in summer the sun rose and set at a place farther to the north. The Sun Watcher, whose task it was to observe this movement, peered through a slit in the Sun Tower at each rising and setting of the sun. On the wall opposite the slit, he made a check against markings which had been scratched into the stone by Sun Watchers long before his time. So the people knew of this movement of the sun northward in summer, and they feared that if it did not check itself, it might desert the earth entirely. In the winter, it moved in the contrary direction and threatened to leave the world buried in snow and ice.

The principal cause of uneasiness, however, was the stories that were told of occasions when the sun disappeared out of the sky entirely. As the people watched in terror it seemed to die by degrees. True, it had always reappeared again, according to these stories, but such occurrences left men's minds with the unhappy feeling that the sun was a living substance, and like all living substances was mortal and was subject to whimsical behavior. Since their own lives, they knew, depended on the sun to warm their bodies and bring growth to their crops, they felt somewhat as children feel toward an elderly parent—they must be respectful and considerate.

Before dawn, runners had gone forth from each of the Seven Clan houses, or kivas. They would visit all the outlying shrines, some of which were at great distances, to place prayer feathers and offerings of sacred meal. They started early, because it was necessary to be back in the village before the sun reached its highest midday point.

Meantime, while the runners were out, officers of each of the Seven Clans took turns marching into the largest plaza, where they danced in two rows. They dressed bravely in many-colored knee-length aprons and sashes, and on their breasts and arms were ornaments of turquoise, shell, feathers, and animal teeth. The costumes were intended

to be gay and bright, to persuade the sun that his earth
children loved him and desired his presence. The songs
they sang were quick and sparkling:

> Behold us here,
> Behold us here,
> Brothers all, ai-ay-ai.
>
> Here we sing,
> Here we sing,
> Brothers all, ai-ay-ai.
>
> Here is food,
> Here is food,
> Brothers all, ai-ay-ai,
> Ai-ay-ai-ai-ai-ai.
>
> Behold us here,
> Behold us here,
> Brothers all, ai-ay-ai.
>
> Here is rest,
> Here is rest,
> Brothers all, ai-ay-ai.
>
> Comes the sun,
> Sparkling sun,
> Brothers all, ai-ay-ai,
> Ai-ay-ai-ai-ai-ai.

The song would go on like that, without stopping, for
several hours, as first one set of singers, then another,
chanted the words. Even the smallest children were en-

couraged to join in these dances and songs, since the sun was fond of children.

As midday approached, the dancers began to leave the central plaza to return to their kivas. People who had been watching, retreated toward their houses. All who could, tried to be out of the direct glare of the midday sun. If a man found himself in the field, he sought a spreading tree or an overhanging rock, there to sit out the sun's climb to its zenith. On this day of the solstice, people waited through the high-noon period for word that the sun had arrived in his northern house and was content not to travel beyond.

The noise of the singing had died away, people everywhere in the village were moving out of sight—then it happened!

First one voice, then several voices, carried the news. The voices came from the far end of the village, toward the south, where the trail came up from the bottom of the canyon. People who had been on the point of entering their houses stopped in their tracks and looked down that way. Others, who were already inside, came out again. No one moved at first, but all stood watching. On a day when people were naturally uneasy, any unexpected happening filled the air with excitement.

Three women had reached the top of the trail and were running toward the village. Their hands were empty of water jars. They were screaming.

"Our spring! Oh, fathers! Our spring!"

As the three women reached the first house, wide-eyed

and panting, other women moved forward in a group and
swallowed them.

"What of the spring? What are you saying?" the women
were asked.

A babble of sound followed. Meantime, other women
were running forward. Men could now be seen standing
in doorways or in the shadow of a building. They watched,
but did not advance.

"What of the spring, Crane Woman?"

The woman thus called by name, eldest of the three,
caught her breath and looked around.

"The spring, my people, is dead," she announced flatly.

The statement shocked everyone into silence. Minds
groped with the words, turned them over and over. How
could a spring die? What kind of nonsense was the woman
talking?

After a moment, everyone talked at once, showering
questions upon the three women. What had they seen?
What happened?

Crane Woman was the first to collect her senses. She
listened for a moment, started to answer a question, then
threw up her hands and demanded silence.

"Peace! Peace! We have no time to stand babbling. The
clan fathers must be told of this at once. Someone go to
each kiva. Tell whomever you find that our spring has
stopped flowing. It exists no more."

"At first, when we arrived to fill our jars, muddy water
was flowing," the second woman explained. She too had
sobered after the battering of questions. "We waited for
it to clear. Then it stopped altogether."

The third woman of the group, hardly more than a girl but already a mother, was the last to speak out. Her voice was still strained. "We waited, and it seemed just to sink into the sand. We were frightened."

By that time, the first men had joined the group, and when they heard these reports they refused to believe them.

"Just wait, now," an old man said. He had a withered right leg and walked with the aid of a thick crutch which his bad leg wrapped itself around. He went by the name of Mountain Walker.

"Our clan fathers should not be disturbed here in the middle of the day. You women should take yourselves inside, away from the sun, instead of spreading this fantastic story about our spring drying up. What would we do without our spring?"

Crane Woman threw back her head. "Father, this is no time to worry about the sun, and if we don't tell this to the kiva leaders at once, we will all be sorry. I tell you, our spring is no more; it is dead, it runs no water. I saw it with my own eyes. These women, too. Ask them! Don't tell us we are spreading a fantasy! Just trot down there yourself, if you like."

"Peace, peace, woman!" the old man pleaded. "Obviously, I cannot trot anywhere. You say it ran dirty water first, then stopped. Perhaps a boulder fell from the cliff and blocked it for a while. It will flow again, just you see. In all our lifetimes, and the lifetimes of our fathers, our spring has never failed us. It cannot fail us now. Here, you young fellows, run down and look. Just see if the water hasn't worked its way around the boulder and started to flow again."

"There was no boulder—" Crane Woman started to protest, then stopped, as if she could not be sure. She looked at her two companions, but they only returned her stare. They could not remember whether they had seen a boulder lying in the stream or not.

"Maybe Mountain Walker is right. Maybe it will flow again," a voice came from the group of women.

"We are wasting time, and the kiva leaders will be angry," Crane Woman insisted, but she did not move away.

Two young men had already detached themselves from the group and were disappearing over the edge of the cliff. They would scramble down the log ladder and race for the bottom of the canyon.

The waiting group did not stand in its uncertainty for long, before men began to emerge from the seven kivas. The men of the Turquoise Clan came first. Some even had parts of their ceremonial dress still attached—anklets of eagle feathers, a kilt of black and red design. One man was absent-mindedly carrying an eagle-wing fan. The startling news had caught them as they were undressing.

Following close upon them, came men from the Water-Reed Clan, the Hawk Clan, the Stone Flute Clan, the Gray Badger Clan, the Yellow Rod Clan, and lastly the Spider Clan. Many of these had been taken by surprise too, since they came daubed with the white clay markings and bits of the ceremonial dress in which they had been performing. They streamed up the kiva ladders and out into the street.

The men of the Spider Clan were slower than the others in reaching the street, and only three came forth. Dark Dealer was not among these, though as War Chief and protector of the clan, he should have been among the first. People of the village did not recall this until later.

Now the houses too were emptying. On every terrace and roof top, women and children and old people gathered in silent clusters. "What is it?" was asked everywhere. No one yet knew, or they would not talk about it. "Something. Just wait," mothers told their young ones.

Star Climber had been in his own Turquoise kiva when the Sun Crier, the man who kept vigilance for the clan and made public announcements, scrambled down the ladder and held a whispered conversation. Whatever he said reached only to the ears of the leaders in the center of the room, but from their startled expressions and sharp exclamations, Star Climber knew that a terrible thing had happened. He had come to the kiva, as a dutiful young man should, to help the elders remove their cumbersome dance costumes and do whatever else was required. It filled him with dismay, therefore, when these sober, meticulous men cast aside costumes without regard and sprang for the kiva ladder. All without saying a word to him.

He climbed to the plaza, not sure in his mind whether to leave the kiva unprotected, but pulled strongly by the desire to know what was happening. He could see men hurrying toward the place where the trail came up from the canyon.

He went forward, staying close to the walls of the buildings along the central street. In a moment he arrived op-

posite the opening which led from the street into the dark
interior of the cave. The sacred turkeys were kept there,
always guarded and a damp, sour odor seemed to blow out
from that dark alleyway. On certain days, in winter especially, when the air in the cave seemed not to stir for weeks
at a time, the smell was so bad that people coughed and
their eyes watered when they got near. They always
hurried to pass it.

Children were warned never to go in that passage, and
Star Climber still remembered the time when he forgot
the warning, or decided to go in without regard to the
warning. He had not explored far within the passage when
a masked figure rushed out of the darkness, bellowing,
and lashing at him with a whip of many thongs. He was
a long time getting over the fright; it left him sick and
trembling in every part of his body. Even after many years
he would not even look in the dark entrance, if he were
alone, for fear of finding himself staring into the dead
eyes of a mask. He hurried away.

At last he reached the fringe of the crowd. The women
had made way for the men pouring up from the kivas, and
all waited at the corner of the last building of the village.
The runners who had been sent into the canyon to verify
the stories told by the three women were just then coming
into view.

The head of the trail was above the village and anyone
coming up from the canyon was immediately visible in the
village. The young men waved their arms and shouted
something which Star Climber at least could not hear

clearly. Then they ran forward and were encompassed by the crowd.

"It is true, O fathers," one gasped. "Our spring has stopped flowing."

His breath gave out, and the second runner continued: "We looked for a boulder or rock slide, but there was nothing. The water—just stopped."

"A few pools still hold water," the first speaker resumed. "I think the women should go with their jars. Before it disappears in the ground."

A profound silence fell upon the crowd. If the sun had fallen out of the clear sky on that equinoctial day, the people could not have been more deeply shocked. The spring was life, as was the sun. To be deprived of either, they knew in their hearts at once, meant the end of life. Without water, where would they go? What would they do? Each man and woman pondered these questions as if they had been passed from mouth to mouth, though no word was uttered.

It was Trailing Cloud, the Sun Watcher of the Turquoise Clan, who broke into the shocked silence. His eyesight was dim and his legs unsteady, but his voice was a firm check on their mounting fear. He spoke as if the future were already clear and he knew what each must do.

"Let a woman from each of the clans go with storage jars and collect the water in the pools. Then see that each family gets a fair share. When the pools have been drained, let men from the clans dig pits in the sand. These may fill by morning. But someone will need to watch, to see that the water does not seep away and that no one takes more than his share."

The elder paused for thought, then resumed. "We must get word at once to the man up there." All looked toward the rock shelter in the cliff, knowing that he meant the Holy One. "Shield will go to him. We will ask his help."

He squinted at the crowd that pressed around him. "I cannot tell who is here. I do not see Eldest Woman. Is she here?"

The men looked over the crowd, then at each other. No one had seen her.

"Then send for her," the old man ordered. A younger woman hurried from the crowd. Eldest Woman had been known to refuse to come at the bidding of a man.

Trailing Cloud's mouth quivered, but he held firm. "Tell the Rain Makers to prepare their prayer sticks and their holy meal. We will go down to the spring and speak for the lives of our people."

All at once his strength failed. "I want to sit down," he rasped irritably. His assistants led him to some stone steps where the street climbed up between houses.

The crowd fell apart then. The Rain Makers of each clan went to their kivas to prepare for the ceremony at the spring. Others could not decide whether to go below and see with their own eyes, or whether to wait. Most of the crowd simply stayed together, saying little, scarcely moving. They stood in the full glare of the midday sun and thought nothing of it.

Women, meanwhile, were arriving with jars of all sizes, including some very large storage jars which when filled would be too heavy for a single person to carry up the trail. These would be left below and water would be dipped from them into smaller vessels. Men with digging tools of sharp sticks and stone hand shovels came out of the houses and started down the trail.

"This may be the end of our ancient village," Trailing Cloud spoke as though from a dream. His kiva leaders, the Fire Chief, Tobacco Chief, and Sand Chief stayed with him. At a little distance, the boy, Star Climber, squatted on his heels. He was fearful of approaching too close to the leaders, because of the dread things he might hear, and equally fearful of not being on hand if they should ask for him.

"The people will survive," the old man went on, held in the grip of his dreaming vision. "But they will have to scatter. Who knows what will become of us? By tonight we will start runners out. They will have to range far and wide, to places we have never been, in search of living water. We know all the waters nearby; they are small streams, not enough for all our people, or they flow for only a short time each year."

Then he shook his head and came back to one thought, from which he never strayed far. Many that day kept returning to the same thought.

"This is strange, indeed. Our spring has never failed us before. In my lifetime, and in my father's lifetime, and I do not know for how long before that, the spring never failed. It almost seems as if someone among us has offended the Cloud People and our Guardian Spirits in some grievous way. But who among us will want to say

who is responsible for such a thing! Who among us understands such things!"

The Rain Makers were now returning, but they were
troubled. For each clan there was a Rain Maker Chief and
two assistants. Now they came with their cedar branches,
their prayer sticks topped with kingfisher feathers, their
pouches filled with water-washed stones, and their reed
flutes. All were together and ready, except for the men
from the Spider Clan. They had waited at the Spider Clan
kiva and finally sent someone to ask for the Rain Chief.
No one could say where he was. The sun was now halfway
across the afternoon sky. What were they to do?

Trailing Cloud rose shakily to his feet. In his heart he
knew that something was very wrong; a chill crept through
his body. But a decision had to be made, and he would
make it. He reached out to find a shoulder for support.

"We will go below," he said in a voice turned weak.
"We will go without Spider Clan, though never before
have we acted without all the clans together. Send word
throughout the village that all are to come below, to pray
for our spring and for our people."

Then he asked again for Eldest Woman, and when it
was reported that she had been sent for and could not be
found, a tremor went through his body. Clearly, it was an
evil day.

Criers called through the village and their voices echoed
back as they spread the word.

The clan leaders went first, and as they filed out of the
village, they began to chant of the Far Reaching One and
the Dawn Sky Woman, for these were the first Beings and

all things came from them. First the clan leaders took up the chant and were heard until, group by group, they started down the log ladder and their voices were lost in the chasm. Then, as people of the village followed after the leaders, they continued the chant, until their voices were also lost. It took some time for the village to empty itself. No one hurried. The people walked in what seemed a reluctant procession, as if their minds already assured them that they would fail in this attempt. Finally, all had departed and their singing came more faintly, echoed back from the far side of the canyon.

The people of the Spider Clan had not joined in the procession, but at the time no one seemed to notice that.

Chapter 10

Water Seeks Its Level

By the time Salt reached the flat country above, day had fully arrived. The sun was at the very edge of the eastern world, resting on the land for a moment before starting his sky walk, and pushing before him giant tree shadows across the land.

Salt remembered his mother's words at morning blessing time—that coyotes would be around that day. It had been owls' talk the first day; then desert doves had called. Now it would be coyotes.

He did not need the warning. Somewhere the enemy waited, behind any pinon tree or crouching boulder. Moving as noiselessly as a shadow, he sped out of the village and up the steep trail to the land above. He paused often to listen and to watch for movement. At those moments of waiting, his hand would move to his chest and the missing turquoise stone—and each time as his hand came away he felt the shock of being alone.

Salt looked carefully around, then crawled to the top of a grassy mound. There he could watch all sides and plan his next move. The land sloped downward toward the planted fields. The fields themselves were hidden behind the ridge that extended eastward from the canyon's edge. In places the ridge consisted of shattered rocks, protruding from the earth like the broken teeth of a monster; elsewhere, the rocks, collapsing entirely, had spilled down the slope in sun-blackened fragments. His eyes came to rest finally at a point along the ridge, where two slabs leaned against each other. These slabs seemed to stand at the top of a heap of loose stone. He had intended to climb those rocks, but the labor of scrambling over the loose gravel had discouraged his curiosity.

He studied the rocks, then turned to other features in the land that stretched out before him. All of it was familiar. All of it had been visited. Today he had to try something, or think of something that he had not tried or thought about before. Tomorrow morning the men would meet in the kiva to perform the wrongway ceremony. If they went through with it, he would have to wait a year before he would be eligible for initiation.

He turned his gaze to the upended slabs of rock and begin to plan how he would move across the terrain. He selected the clumps of pinon and the sheltering rocks he would move to, in succession, when he left his sheltered post. If he went carefully, keeping under cover, crawling like brother-snake when he had to cross open space, and if luck were with him, he might make it without being observed; there would be no coyote cries. It was possible, of course, that an arrow would find his back and no sound be heard. Not by his ears.

Once more he looked carefully, then slid down the grassy hill and reached the first grove of pinon trees. There he waited, while he tried to decide whether the birds had been disturbed. He listened for a song broken off too suddenly, or an unusually long interval between bursts of song, a warning that he was not alone in the land. But if another was present, he too remembered the habits of birds.

Walking, crawling, he reached the next pinon shelter, then ran between the sheltering banks of a dry stream bed. The sun was well into the sky when finally he came to the last protective cover. The ridge then lay just in front of him and the ground between lay barren of any growth. A body moving up that exposed surface would be seen.

Day advanced and he could wait no longer. No arrow yet, no coyote cry. Finding hopefulness in this, he rose among the low-growing junipers where he had been crouching, and ran like the nimble-footed deer. Even when the ground rose sharply and he found himself among a waste of loose rocks, he still ran. His breath came in gasps, his heart seemed about to burst through his chest, but he bounded from footing to footing until he reached the top of the ridge. He looked back. Amazing, the distance he had covered and the height he had reached!

The planted fields lay directly before him now, on the other side of the ridge; and to the west, which was to his left as he reached the summit, he could see the edge of the canyon. The village was below, out of sight.

He did not know that at this moment, as he looked at the sky space above the village, disaster awaited his people. If he had known what was happening that morning, he might have understood why no one had attempted to ambush him. His fears would have seemed foolish, swallowed up in an anxiety greater than anything he had imagined.

The upended rock slabs rose massive, now that he stood at their base. Wind and frost had battered them and sent chips and splinters showering down the sloping sides. What remained was still a mighty thrust of brown and golden rock standing taller than any pine tree.

Salt began a careful study of the rock giants. He crawled over large detached boulders, already scorching hot. By midday, with the sun straight overhead, the heat of those rocks would be unbearable. He had to find what he wanted, and get out. But what did he seek?

The old people had a saying: "Looking for what you want but can't find, is like looking for the hole in the wind."

The entrance to the secret trail *had* to be in the land

above the canyon. But that was all he knew. The sun burned his flesh and sweat trickled from under his hair and down his face and neck, where it dried in trails of salt.

These rocks must hold the answer; he had sought everywhere else. In all the country lying below the ridge, hardly a tree or rock or clump of yucca had been missed. He had crisscrossed the earth, running in long, jolting strides and listening for the rumbling sound of a hollow place beneath the surface; he had thumped the boles of pinon trees and crashed rocks against larger boulders. Without avail.

The more he thought about these spires of rock, these teeth of the monster, the more certain he felt that this time he would find more than the hole in the wind. Working his way around the base of the first rock, he searched each crack and fault, and studied with special care the point at which the naked stone emerged from the surrounding rubble.

Finally, he arrived at the western face of the spire, where it was split at the base. From a distance this split gave the spire the appearance of two rock slabs leaning against each other. The appearance was false. It was all one mass, pyramid-shaped, but material had broken away from the inner side, leaving a hollow shell.

Then something checked his growing excitement. He was looking down into a depression at the base of the rock spire. The overhanging rock blocked out the sun, leaving the bottom of the depression in deep shadow. Almost at the bottom, he saw the stretched-out form of a man. He did not need to go nearer to know the man was dead.

The second shock came immediately. He crept down

the sloping stone. Then stopped. It was Flute Man. A club or a heavy stone had crushed his head; and this had happened some hours before.

Long ago Salt had learned to use his eyes. Two things explained what had happened. Flute Man had not been killed on the spot, for he had not bled here. And beside the body lay a long torch made from a lightning-killed pinon tree. Such wood was pitch-laden and burned brightly. The torch had been used, either by Flute Man or by those who had carried him to this place. This suggested an underground cave or passage, where a light was needed.

One more thing he saw, but the meaning was not clear. On Flute Man's breast lay an owl's claw, imbedded in feathers. Whether Flute Man had been killed by someone claiming the powers of witchcraft, or whether Flute Man was himself accused of witchcraft, Salt could not tell. He did not touch the evil object.

Almost immediately he found the trail. Even so, he might have missed it, if he had not expected it to be near. No one liked to touch the dead, and therefore Flute Man had not been carried far. But at first, as he sought, Salt seemed to face nothing but rock; the solid rock of the walls that rose above him, and shattered fragments lying in heaps. Still he continued his search. He turned over boulders that might be used to plug a hole, he tapped stone walls for hollow sounds.

Suddenly he knew that he had been staring for a long time at the answer. The rock, which had fallen away from the inner side of the spire, had left a narrow ledge running across the face of the break. This ledge was high, at least the height of two men. But on close examination he saw that in the wall were obvious hand- and footholds. When he tried them, they were perfectly spaced for climbing. He returned to the body of Flute Man and picked up the pinon torch.

The sun, now at the mid-point of the sky, poured relentless heat upon the exposed rocks. Salt reached up to the first handhold, climbed.

The narrow ledge, barely offering space for a man's body, sloped downward to the left. The footing was precarious. Salt leaned sharply inward, his hands raised above his head, his palms flat against the hot stone. Thus he moved sideways along the rock face. At the lower end of the ledge, where it beveled down to the outer edge of the spire, he observed a narrow space between the main body of rock and a lesser slab. This slab, fracturing away, had fallen back against the larger mass. A man could just squeeze through the narrow opening.

He had found what he had come for . . . and with swelling heart he thought of how he could report to the Holy One. He looked back where the sunlight burned so fiercely over the ground he had covered. Flat faces of rock shot the blinding sun back into his eyes. He smiled at how he had worried out there in the sun; how he had run here and there.

He turned from the view, and as he stooped to explore the opening, he remembered something else. The Holy One had told him: "You are starting something which may end with giving your life." The words, sounding in memory,

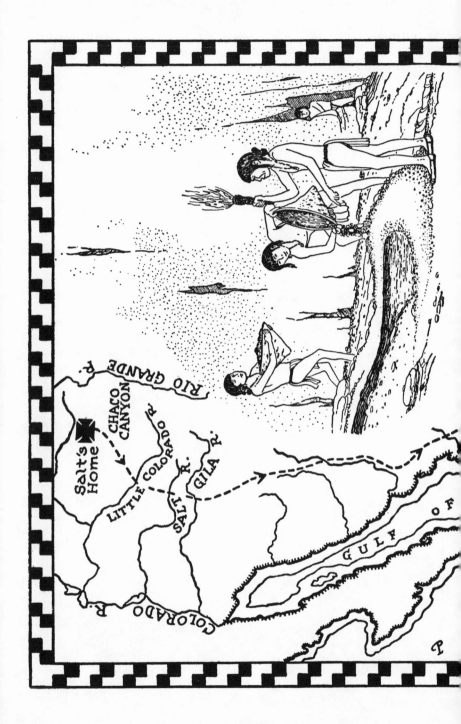

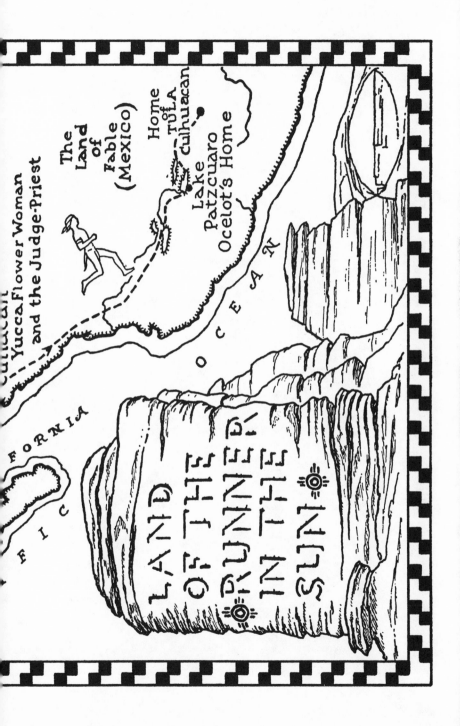

choked off the elation which rose like bird song in his throat.

"But what could happen now?" he heard himself whisper. "The arrow was shot out there in the open. The rock fell as I climbed the cliff. Here I am safe from watching eyes."

No voice was there to answer, else he might have learned that the secret trail was already discovered and invaded. What generations of his people had guarded carefully, was secret no more. And the same voice might have persuaded him that wisdom and safety lay in retreat, rather than in advancing. Because he knew nothing of the occurrence at the spring, and in his ignorance pushed forward into the unknown, he almost failed his people.

For Dark Dealer, the days of angry waiting were ending.

He had said to his clansmen: "Look to me, I will make our Spider Clan powerful! *We* will decide who lives in this village and who goes."

Before he became War Chief of Spider Clan, Dark Dealer had accomplished little that was either good or bad. His family had not been large. It might be said he belonged to no one. He ate wherever he found himself at mealtime. No household would turn a child away from food, but with him it was more than courtesy. His mother, a small, waspish person, was always quarreling with her neighbors and scolding her three children. Out of pity for the boy and his two sisters, other households took them in and showed them kindness.

As War Chief, new energies seemed to be released in
this man who was nobody's child. Impatient in kiva meetings, he succeeded after a while in compelling his clansmen
to abandon many of the courteous customs which governed
such meetings. He would state what was to be discussed
and who was to speak, and if he was displeased with a
meeting, he broke it up. He had won over a group of
younger men by favors and promises, and when he decided
that a meeting had gone far enough and he wanted it
ended, he gave the nod and the young men talked in loud
tones, laughed, called out insulting words when anyone
tried to speak, until peaceful men gave up in disgust.

But Dark Dealer's greatest weapon lay in witchcraft.
The village lived in great fear of sickness, since sickness
often struck without warning. It brought pain and even
death. It might go away, too, but not one could tell whether
sickness when it came would destroy a man or let him go.
It was easy to believe that sickness was caused by unseen
powers striking back at an individual who broke some rule
of conduct. But if a man searched his mind and could find
no wrongdoing, then he worried. He would think over
who might be his enemies, who might wish him evil, and
if he concluded that someone had used evil power against
him, fear would enter his mind and he might become sick
indeed.

Many were the ways of using evil power. When a man
cut his hair, he was careful to bury the cuttings secretly;
otherwise they might fall into the hands of a witch. Bones
that remained from a meal must be thrown into the fire.
Danger could come from an article of clothing or an orna-

ment lost or misplaced outside of a man's home. Any personal possession, falling into unfriendly hands, could be used to destroy the owner.

Dark Dealer knew these things, and more.

When, after two candidates had already met untimely deaths, he proposed himself as War Chief, he hardly expected to be accepted. He was still young, he had accomplished nothing. He made his proposal to the Chief of the Summer House, it being the period of the year when authority over all political affairs of the clan was held by that chief. The expected rejection followed. The Summer Chief, a man called Echo, was polite but definite in his reaction.

"It pleases me that you offer yourself. I thought these matters did not interest you."

Dark Dealer considered. The two stood alone just outside the Spider Clan kiva. Afternoon brightness had faded and long slanting shadows reached across the canyon. In the distance children played a singing game.

"Why do you say I am not the right one, when my mother is of the same family as that of the last War Chief?"

The tone of the other was still firm. "That is a point in your favor. But to be War Chief, you need to be older. The people need to know what you can do. It requires much learning besides."

"I can learn as well as anyone else."

"No doubt. Still . . . up to now, you *haven't* learned."

The more firmly the Summer Chief spoke against him, the more decided became Dark Dealer's ambitions. Moreover, he had prepared himself for the interview. So he posed a question:

"The other two who were considered, and who died as soon as they were named . . . might it not be that they were not the right ones, after all?"

"What do you say? I do not understand."

"To be War Chief, a man must be able to destroy. If he is destroyed instead, clearly he does not have the power needed by the people."

"Perhaps so. Do you have this power?"

"The one who fell over the cliff . . . I can show you a strand of his hair. The other, killed by lightning . . . I can show you his sandal. And you, Uncle, you lost the shells which you use to pluck the hair from your face. I will return these shells, if you like."

The Summer Chief was thunderstruck. His hand reached for the skin pouch at his belt, then halted. He had known for several days that these shells were missing; he had been troubled by the loss. He saw Dark Dealer in quite a new light and continued to stare at him for some moments. It had grown dusk by then, but the elder man, Echo, saw enough.

So it happened that Dark Dealer was named War Chief.

That success led to bolder ventures, until in time he convinced himself and his followers that he could take over the leadership of the entire village. He discovered, as he went along, that the men who held positions of authority in his clan were not able to fight him. They had been taught by their seniors to do things in a certain way. Any other way seemed wrong, but they had no reasons in support of the old way, except that it had been taught them. Dark Dealer found that when he ignored the old men, or acted in a manner contrary to old practices, they were helpless. They grumbled, but they did nothing.

Then he made a discovery which opened the way for domination of the entire Village of the White Rocks.

The discovery grew out of an idle question. One of the younger men had asked in a kiva meeting: "I wonder what is back of the wall where the sacred turkeys are kept?"

Dark Dealer answered.

"What wall? And why shouldn't there be a wall? To make a room you build a wall."

"But this wall," the young man answered, "is not part of a room. The turkeys are kept in an open space between buildings. Guards stand in front to keep the creatures from getting into the street and keep anyone else from getting into them. The rear of the space should be the cliff itself. But instead, a wall of fitted stones is built across, blocking the passage to the cliff."

"How do you know this? The guards will not let anyone through there."

The young man, who was called Open Face, saw that Dark Dealer was interested, which was what he wanted.

"It is nothing," he said and gestured to signify nothing. "One of the guards likes to sleep; if you watch him, you can manage it."

"The place has such a bad smell, who would want to go in there? It is probably nothing. Some guard built the wall while he had nothing to do."

Open Face had no intention of stopping at that. "I

thought it was nothing, until I went in there. The guard stirred in his sleep, so I crouched down to keep in shadow. My head was against the wall. I heard footsteps, and thought they were in the street, or perhaps in one of the houses nearby. They were faint at first, then they seemed to come near. Finally they stopped. After a while I heard other steps. I heard voices. Even a name was spoken."

Dark Dealer leaned forward. "A name? What name?"

"I think it was Day Singer. That was how it sounded."

"Day Singer!"

The name was enough. It meant that the Turquoise Clan had a secret behind the rock wall; Dark Dealer would not let the matter rest until he knew that secret.

It was easy to dispose of the guard, who belonged to the Turquoise Clan. Dark Dealer appeared one day, when no one was within earshot, and threatened to expose the guard as a witch. The man protested angrily that he would break any man's head who claimed he was a witch. He had been seated on a stone bench just inside the entrance to the turkey pens. The shocking accusation brought him to his feet.

"I am glad to hear you say that," Dark Dealer answered, as if he had been made quite happy. "It shows that you realize what a serious matter it is to go around with witches, or to be one yourself. I have been told that you carry an owl's claw in your belt pouch. If the one who told me this is wrong, I will denounce him myself. So open your pouch and prove that you are innocent."

The guard did not hesitate. He plucked the pouch from his belt, opened it; and there was the owl's claw!

His eyes bulged and the pouch fell to the ground. "How can it be? I never saw it before!"

Dark Dealer dropped his pretense of pleasantness. "So! Just what I was told! You never saw it before! Miserable liar! A lucky thing for our village that you are discovered. Now I can tell the criers to warn the people."

The guard, a big man, was stupefied. He looked steadily at the object on the ground and seemed to pay no attention to Dark Dealer's words. Yet he must have heard, for presently he protested: "It is a lie."

"When I tell about you, the people won't listen to your excuses. It will be the end for you."

The guard looked up. His eyes searched the man facing him. He had begun to guess at the truth of what had happened, but he said nothing.

Dark Dealer continued. "But I want to be your friend, and I will make a bargain. I will save your life, if you will help me."

The guard was convinced then that he had been tricked. Still he said nothing.

"There is a stone wall back here. I want you to help me make an opening in that wall so I can get through and see what is on the other side."

At that, the guard's anger exploded. He hurled himself forward and, with a mighty blow, sent Dark Dealer reeling across the entranceway. It was a blow struck in vain. Three young men who had been concealed just outside, rushed in and subdued the angry man. One was ready to club him, after the other two had pinned his arms behind his back, but Dark Dealer interfered.

"My friend made a mistake," he said. He gasped noisily through a bloody mouth, but tried to make his voice sound natural. "He is going to help us. He knows what happens to witches. Don't you, friend?"

Gaining access to the secret trail made easy everything that followed, though at first Dark Dealer did not realize the value of his discovery. He could understand the trail as a means of escape, but that was of no use unless the village was under attack. His first conclusion was that the Turquoise men had kept the trail secret to save their own members in case of enemy attack.

Only after he had explored the full length of the trail, was he able to appreciate what power had come into his hands.

The trail ran underground, from the innermost part of the cave to the outlet among the rock spires. Originally it was an underground water channel. The rocky ridge, at some far distant time, had thrust upward as a molten mass through the surrounding sandstone. When the rock cooled, it was quite hard, much harder than the sandstone, and it lay like a great dike across the land. Waters flowing along the surface of the earth were stopped by the dike, and at one time a great lake had formed behind the rock barrier. Thousands of years later, Salt's people planted their fields in this old lake bed, rich in silt.

Water is always hungry; it is always eating away at earth and rock, and if it finds a crack it will soon make a chasm. The water in the ancient lake, finding a soft spot where the sandstone had been split by the erupting volcanic rock, seeped downward, eating its way by dissolving the surrounding material, always seeking a lower-flowing level. At one time the underground channel emptied into the cave of the White Rocks, then spilled over into the canyon in a great splashing waterfall.

Long before Salt's ancestors moved to the cave, the waterfall had ceased to exist. The first people saw no sign that water had ever flowed through the cave; boulders and rock trash had fallen from the ceiling and buried the channel. The water, always hungry, had found another soft spot along its underground course and worked its way to a lower-flowing level. In time it emerged at the bottom of the canyon as the bubbling spring which the people called sacred, and praised in song and legend. It meant life; it meant the end of wandering.

Water no longer flowed on the surface, in the flat country among the planted fields. But it seeped down from the far mountains, it crawled through the gravels that lay beneath the surface, and when it came to the volcanic dike, it was diverted as of old into the channel under the old lake bed, and emerged in the spring at the bottom of the canyon. The volume of water had been decreasing in late years and that was cause for worry; but so long as the spring flowed at all the people felt secure.

Dark Dealer and his young men had an imperfect understanding of what had happened in the underground region, but it was easy enough to see, by the aid of their smoking pinon torches, that an underground stream flowed at their feet and disappeared, with a roar, into a black abyss. Damp rocks gleamed in the torchlight like a thousand watchful eyes, and dampness filled the air. It was a frightening place, and when they came upon it, they were terrified. Dark Dealer was the first to approach for a closer view. He even handed his torch to one of his companions while he threw boulders into the yawning pit. His thought was to discover how deep was the hole. But he heard only the thunder of the rushing water.

That night, when he was back in the village and heard the women in his own household complain that the spring water had turned muddy during the afternoon, he began to understand what had happened.

The next day he returned, walking past a guard whose eyes burned fear and hatred, and threw more boulders into the roaring pit. One of his men was stationed at the spring, and by comparing notes afterward they were able to tell almost exactly how long it took the water to flow from the secret trail to the spring.

In a matter of days, Dark Dealer had worked out the plan which was to place himself and his Spider Clan in possession of the Village of the White Rocks.

Chapter 11

The Ambush

SALT, crawling from the hot midday sun into the dark opening in the rocks, realized that he had acted foolishly. In his excitement he had pushed through the outer cleft in the rock, and found that the opening widened and was high enough for him to stand erect. When he spread his arms, he could barely touch the rock walls. This pleased him. But then the passage narrowed; as he stooped to wedge his head and shoulders into the opening, he discovered that the passage took a sharp downward pitch.

He stayed for some time on his knees, trying to see into the slanting shaft. Since his body blocked out the light he stared into darkness. He knew that he must crawl into the black hole, and he hesitated. Darkness was an enemy that could attack at any time, from any side. Only a prodding sense of what was expected forced him at last to crawl into the passage. He stopped after a moment and lay still, hoping that his eyes would adjust themselves and he might see what lay ahead. But this was hopeless; he must depend entirely on his hands to guide him down into this darkness.

After a few feet, the space became so cramped he could not free the pinon torch on which he was lying. The weight of his body wedged the torch securely and he could not move it. When he tried to reverse himself and crawl backward, the steep angle stopped him.

It had been foolish, he thought, lying there, not to have lighted the torch before he started. Not only was the thick pine wood now useless to him, but it dug into his ribs, wedging him into a space already too narrow.

And now, a further concern—how could he be sure that he had found the right opening? He had crawled into the first hole he saw; perhaps there was another. This one seemed to get narrower with every inch he moved forward. Would he wedge himself hopelessly between jagged rocks and never again see daylight?

"What you are starting may end with giving your life." Was that what the Holy One meant? That he would die right here in this black tunnel?

Thought of the Holy One brought other thoughts. Would all this trouble in the kiva have started, he wondered, if he had not planted corn in the canyon? Asking this of himself, he remembered vividly the pleasant days down there, when between planting and tending his secret corn, he would race in the sun and hurl his curved stick at a bounding rabbit. No thought to kill on those occasions, only the enjoyment of feeling the tug on his throwing muscles.

Memory darkened then, as he heard the Holy One rebuke him for planting that very corn. What was meant in his saying, "Our corn suffers from something more than want of water"? What would be revealed?

In his vexation, he drove hard to free himself and move forward, deeper into the black uncertainty. His body broke into sweat, yet he was chilled.

The passage dipped downward still more sharply. Presently he faced a new problem. The tunnel had grown larger again; his body no longer touched its sides. But now, because it was so steep, he began to slide. When he struck out for a handhold, a jagged point slashed the flesh, and he jerked back. He dared not rise to his knees; he might not hold his balance, and would fall face downward. His belt caught on an unevenness in the floor, holding him for an instant. He moved cautiously, trying to turn sidewise, to find some way to brace himself.

But the angle was too steep. He slipped, and this time went plunging on, down the steep incline. It was a moment when courage meant nothing; duty meant nothing. This being taken by surprise, with no chance to help himself, filled him with despair.

His plunge ended in a clatter of loose stones; clouds of

bitter dust struck his eyes and filled his mouth. He rolled over several times and heard himself groan. For several moments he lay without moving, as he waited for courage to return.

Then he sat up. He was bruised and scratched; his hands seemed to be bleeding. But that didn't matter. A sound so unexpected caught his attention that every other sensation was lost.

It was the sound of water flowing, whispering as it coursed over rocks and into little pools. He heard it clearly. In the blackness, he even imagined that he saw clear water running over bright pebbles. It was like human speech; a familiar thing in a world of blackness and confusion.

He crawled a few feet to the edge of the stream and bathed his hands in the ice-cold water, nor did he mind the sting of the water on the lacerated flesh. He put his mouth to the water and drank deeply. Cautiously he rose, first to his knees, then to his full height. The discovery that he could stand erect still further renewed his courage. His shivering ceased. All he now needed was light!

It took some moments of prowling on hands and knees to locate the pine torch. He found it at last, not in the loose gravel at the bottom of the steep incline, but partway up; it had lodged itself crosswise in the passageway.

Then something happened which brought back all the fear he had felt in the black of the tunnel. With the fire rocks and tinder from his belt pouch he was preparing to start a blaze to ignite his pine torch. It was not easy to arrange these materials in the dark, and he spent some moments finding a level spot and laying out the tinder where sparks from the flint rocks would be sure to fall upon it. He also carried short splinters of pitch to pick up the flame from the tinder, and these had to be placed where his fingers could find them quickly. As he worked carefully with these materials, he glanced up.

At first Salt could not believe what he saw. He sat back on his haunches and stared, thinking that, whatever it was, it would go away. It did not go away, so he picked up the materials he had laid out and put them back in the pouch. He did this without thinking, in a daze.

What he saw was a glow of light, like feeble torchlight, rising and falling; but so commonplace an explanation seemed impossible. Salt's world was a world of witches; they were a part of everyday conversation; they came and went according to mysterious ways, with the power to corrupt and to destroy. A cry that was an echo out of his childhood escaped him. Surely, he had fallen into the underground home of the witch people!

For a moment, when it seemed as if the light was coming toward him, he thought wildly of scrambling back up the tunnel. But standing, he forced himself to face the light. It was still there, its feeble glow still rose and fell gently. He decided, after a moment, it was not coming any nearer. Whatever the source, it was far away, like faint lightning flashing below the horizon.

A weak and wavering confidence returned to him, though he was baffled. He knew himself to be in the secret trail, which only the Holy One and two others in the village knew about. How could there be a light, unless a hand was there to make it? And whose would be the hand? Those sworn to keep the secret of the trail—or some other?

The urge to turn and run shook him powerfully. He wanted to be back in the sunlight! Only he dared not report to the Holy One that he had seen a strange light and had been frightened. He dared not ask to be returned to his place among the men, when he had not carried out the task given him.

Once more he faced the flickering light. He began moving down the trail; half crouching, feeling through his moccasins for loose stones and obstructions. The sound of the whispering water journeyed with him; the voice of a friend, there in the darkness.

The light was farther away than he had judged, and he walked for some time before he seemed to come any nearer. The sound of voices halted him at last. Men were speaking, but so far away he could only guess he heard speech; he could not make out any words. He squatted on his heels and waited, listening for a footfall. Soon he heard the sound again, and was more certain that it was human speech. Again he waited, until he was satisfied that the speakers were not coming toward him.

He rose and moved ahead, crouching, and feeling still more carefully for stones that might rattle underfoot. The light was stronger now. Patterns of light and shadow reflected back from the roof of the tunnel, which now stood higher than his outstretched arms could reach. The stream, dropping down over shelves of rock into little pools, looked black in the reflected light.

He rounded a bend in the trail, and dropped flat. He had almost walked into the middle of a group of men, some of whom held pine torches high above their heads, while others moved with burdens on their backs.

Salt observed, as soon as he dared lift his head, that the tunnel had opened into a wide, low-ceilinged cavern, irregular in shape. The torches flared and fell, sending up great clouds of smoke. In this uncertain light it was hard to tell how wide the room was or how far ahead it extended. Brown-skinned men moved in and out of shadow. Salt trembled as he watched them, still inclined to think of them as creatures belonging to another world. When he recognized the speech of his own people and saw familiar faces, he almost ran forward to join them. Luckily, he stayed low. Some instinct told him that he had moved from unknown fears into certain danger, that he was facing desperate men.

The little stream had now turned into a lake. Lights glinted on a surface of water. As he continued to watch, lying in shadow, he noticed that the men with burdens were actually loaded down with carrying-baskets, filled with rock and dirt. They were transporting this material downstream, from the place where he had almost stumbled upon them, and depositing it in the stream bed—building a dam. They were hurrying, constantly trotting, from the bank where they scooped up the material, to the dike downstream which rose several feet above the surface of the water. He could hear their gasping breaths, echoed back from the low ceiling.

He could not understand the purpose of the labor.

Building a dam here in the underground would flood the secret trail—but why? He realized, unhappily, that he must creep closer. He must get a better view of what these men were doing; perhaps their talk would explain their action. Only when he had done this could he make a useful report to the Holy One.

While seeking some way to advance, he almost changed his mind. The torches flickered uncertainly and sent up clouds of smoke, but the light was still strong enough to reach into the deepest nooks and corners. Shadow and light chased each other back and forth across the low chamber. It seemed impossible for anyone to creep any closer and not be discovered.

Then watching for some time, he discovered that the four torchbearers never looked behind. They held their torches aloft to guide the burden bearers as they came with their empty baskets; and the men carrying the baskets, because of the light that shone in their eyes, could scarcely see behind the torchbearers. Each was intent on his own task, with thought only for that.

Salt waited for the right moment, when the burden bearers had filled their baskets and were trotting downstream, then he slipped over the ground, keeping close to the sandstone wall. The torchbearers turned downstream with extended arms, their bodies producing a vague and faltering shadow. He inched forward, then lay still. Head down, he watched only the pebbles and stones in front of him. At any moment might come a cry of discovery.

About half the distance between his starting place and the dike the trail curved to the left, away from the water.

The underground chamber broadened out into a kind of bay, not visible from where he first watched. Should he follow the wall of the chamber, retreating from the scene of action, or stay close to the torchbearers and risk discovery? He had already passed two men, but the other two were ahead.

Then he made a further discovery.

As he raised his head to study his next move, he saw what he took to be the bodies of two dead men. They were trussed securely with thongs of hide. Why, if they were dead, were they bound? The bodies lay in shadow, away from the dike. He moved in that direction.

He was still some distance away, crawling painfully over jagged rocks, when he realized that one of the bound men was Day Singer. The second man, Turtle, was someone Salt knew only casually, and he did not recognize him now. He might not have recognized Day Singer, so badly was he beaten about the face, but his was a familiar form and manner of dress.

Now, more than ever, Salt sensed the nearness of danger. Some terrible thing had happened, and he was caught in it. The realization hit him hard, and for a moment he could not move at all.

It was thought of Day Singer that stirred him again. When he had crawled closer and found the men breathing, he felt better. But now he had the problem of what to do. The men were too badly hurt to help themselves even if he succeeded in cutting their bonds. He would need help to set them free. But how could he risk leaving Day Singer and Turtle while he went for help?

As he lay puzzling about this, he failed to notice a
shadow detaching itself from the background of shadow
behind him. And when the club came down on his head,
he saw only a burst of light, but felt no pain.

Neither did he hear a heavy voice speak out a moment
later:

"Carry him and the other two below to the kiva. They
will decide down there what to do with so many nosey
people. Here, our work is finished."

Chapter 12

Dark Dealer Takes Command

THE SUN had already passed beyond the far rim, and deepening shadow was moving up from the bottom of the canyon when chanting voices were again heard. Prayers had been said at the spring and the people were returning up the trail. Each in his heart was thinking that this day of the solstice had been a day of disaster. They thought of their homes, where fires should already be burning but had not even been lighted, and wondered how long they would be able to remain in the

141

security they had known. Without water, it could not be for long. But where would they go? That was a question never out of their minds.

They came up the trail in the same order in which they went from the village—first the clan leaders, followed by the older men, then the older women; then young families, man and wife; then the children. And as they came up the trail, they were again chanting of the Far Reaching One and the Dawn Sky Woman.

Suddenly the procession stopped. Turquoise Clan men, led by Trailing Cloud, the Sun Watcher, and his four assistants, had reached the walls of the first buildings, where the long central street began.

They stopped before a barricade of rocks, built from wall to wall, blocking the street completely.

Trailing Cloud, walking slowly and with bent head, came to the barricade; he almost fell against it, before he realized that it was there. His white hair made a faint glow in the gathering darkness.

He stopped, then put out his hand, thinking that his failing eyesight had played him a trick. But the stones were there, just as his eyes had observed them. He looked around for the men at his side.

"What is it? What has happened?" he asked, as if arousing from a dream.

The others had been looking, too. They saw the wall, saw that it rose to the height of two men and looked most solid, but what it was or how it came to be there they could not explain.

"We cannot say, brother," Between Feathers answered.

He was Fire Tender in the kiva. "It was not here before. Now it is here."

"It was built to keep us out of the village," the Sand Chief growled. "But who could do it? We all went to pray at the spring."

Farther back in the crowd, which by then had massed close against the barricade, a woman's voice spoke out: "Where were your eyes, old men, if you thought everybody went to the spring? I looked, and saw not a single man, woman, child or dog from the Spider Clan. They stayed up here while we went to pray—they are the ones who are taking our homes."

The speaker was Crane Woman, one of the three women who had discovered the failing spring.

At these words, spoken with rising anger, laughter came from above. All heads turned and all eyes gazed upward. Then all knew what had happened.

Dark Dealer stood on the roof top, looking down. His laughter was not of the kind that rises out of pleasure or gives pleasure.

"One at least among you is clever enough to understand a simple thing. No surprise to me that a woman should see it first. You Turquoise men are too blind to be of any use to yourselves—or any use to our village. Now that is ended."

The same laughter slashed through the words.

"The woman is right. This is now the village of the Spider Clan. The houses are our houses. We will divide the kivas among our societies. We always needed space." The voice trailed off. In the following silence, men heard their own breathing.

"Well! Aren't you going to object? You, Trailing Cloud! I see no other leader among you. You are deserted. What have you to say?"

The old Sun Watcher took a step forward. He stood quite alone. He wore a loose shirt of white cotton that covered him to his knees, with a red sash around his waist. His failing eyes could not take in the man who taunted him, but sight was not needed—the fading light caught itself in his white hair and glowed for a moment.

"We are not without our leaders," the words came thin and sharp from the old man. "You will reckon with them before this time is passed."

"You think so, old man? And what will they feast on, these leaders? What food and water have they stored up for the fools who will follow them?"

Trailing Cloud's head was tilted upward as if his eyes really saw—his infirm muscles had found the strength to hold him without faltering.

"We have stored up peace in our hearts, something you have forgotten. Men may die for want of food and water, and death is miserable. But would it not be more miserable for us if, through fear of death, we yielded to you? You must know, since you were born among us, that when our Mother Corn came to our elders, we were told to keep peace in our minds and in all our actions. Those who remember this and live accordingly will never be destroyed. If you forgot to take this into account when you captured our houses and our food, I remind you of it now. We will survive, will we not?" The old man turned with the words to face the men and women crowding close behind him. "Will we not?"

The crash of many voices echoed against the inner wall of the cavern and rolled out across the canyon: "We will take care of ourselves. We spit upon this traitor!"

The words were like a whiplash across the face of Dark Dealer. He had enjoyed the taunts he threw down at the massed bodies. Now, he would sting them. Now, he would show who was master.

He turned to others who until then had not been visible.

"They speak of their leaders. Good! Bring one of them here. Let them see for themselves."

The crowd below could not observe what was happening, but men moved across the roof, dragging something with them. They approached Dark Dealer with their burden. He reached down, and when he straightened up again, an anguished gasp rose from the crowd below.

Dark Dealer had placed his foot on the low parapet that ran along the roof. With one hand he pulled Eldest Woman into view, holding her by the hair for them to see. Her eyes were closed in death.

"Here is one who stood against me. Here is one of your leaders. Will you be next, old man, down there? Look, I give her back to you!" With that, he rolled the body over the parapet. It fell clumsily over the heaped rocks and came to rest at the feet of Trailing Cloud.

Cries of amazement changed into shouts of anger. "We can't stand for this! See what he has done! The man must be destroyed! Destroy him!"

The shouting died suddenly. The leader on the roof had summoned his young men to his side, and they appeared armed with bows, lances, and war clubs.

A fresh outburst of laughter from Dark Dealer.

"You see? You forgot your weapons when you left your houses. My men collected them from every hiding place. If you want to attack us, we will be happy to shoot you down with your own arrows."

Trailing Cloud turned to his people. "He speaks a terrible truth. While we prayed for our village, even for these thieves, they were destroying us. There is nothing for us to do but take our beloved Eldest Woman away from here and make a grave for her. Then we shall see. The day has not ended."

Above the grumbling of many voices rose that of Crane Woman: "But what are we to do? Our food is in there, in our houses. Our children are hungry."

"Peace, woman," Trailing Cloud answered in a voice dazed with anger and weariness. "We must get away from here and talk among ourselves. We must make plans. The Holy One will be with us, I promise you."

"But where? Where is he?" Crane Woman insisted. "You asked Shield to go for him. Where are they?"

The people were beginning to move, all unwillingly, when the voice called to them from the roof top once more.

"Why do you hurry? Wouldn't you like to know what plans I have for our village?"

"What plans can he have but to murder us all?" asked Crane Woman.

No one would have lingered, so hateful had become

that voice. Yet the people could not move away. As they talked among themselves they cast angry glances at the man on the roof, who seemed to wait at his ease, knowing they would listen to him. It did not ease their humiliation to realize that they could do nothing. To try to climb the wall of rock with armed men shooting down into them meant certain death, and defeat. Even so, the younger men would try it and came crowding forward amid cries of "No! No! Stop them!"

So the people milled about in that narrow upward trail. Children, big-eyed with fear, pressed against their mothers. Some whimpered, but were silenced when a mother put her hand over a trembling mouth.

The watchers on the roof had built up a fire, which threw a feeble, wavering light over the watching faces below. It was full dark when Trailing Cloud called back to Dark Dealer.

"The choice is not ours, so we will listen. What have you to say to us?"

"A simple thing." The voice seemed so free of trickery, the listeners marveled at the shamelessness. "A simple thing," he repeated. "You saw the spring die today—the spring which gives life to your children and to all of us. Is that not enough to persuade you that the men who have been leaders in our village have lost their power? Who can say what wrongful thing they have done? Certainly a wrong was committed, or we would not be punished in this way. I accuse no one, but I ask each of you to think about it. Who is our Village Chief? Where does he live? Can he be found in the village, where he is needed? Can our mothers and our children and our clan leaders go to him in time of trouble?"

He waited, but not for answers to his questions. He would convince them, if he could, that he was an elder brother, concerned with their comfort and safety.

"Where your Village Chief has failed you, I can protect you. I can bring back the water to the spring. Do you hear? Do you believe me? I can make the spring flow again."

He paused, but there was no silence. Instead, many voices broke into sounds of surprise, disbelief, mockery.

"What trick is this?" asked a voice from the darkness.

"We waste our time listening to him," the Sand Chief growled. "He cares nothing for us or for our village."

"Wait!" Trailing Cloud spoke. "Whether we trust his words or not, we must hear him. Stay and listen." He turned to face Dark Dealer, on whom the firelight flickered. "You speak of bringing the water back to the spring. How can you do this? How are we to know that you can do it?"

"I can do it because I have the power. I tell you nothing beyond that. But this I tell you." The voice on the roof top turned wrathful, as though the patience of a just man had come to an end. "This I will tell you—you no longer deal with a fool. You no longer deal with foolish old men who have outlived their usefulness. When I tell you that my power can bring the water back to the spring, I know whereof I speak.

"Now! I will cause the spring to flow again. On one condition. Bring the Holy One here before me. I shall be named Village Chief. In the presence of all of you, he shall name me to that office. The altar which is in his keeping shall be turned over to me. The shrines which he protects, and all the duties which he performs, shall be turned over to me. You will witness these things, and you will approve. Spider Clan shall be the first clan in the village, going before all others in our village ceremonies. These things you will approve. And when this has been done, the water will flow again in the spring. All this can come to pass before Sun, our Father, rises from his morning bed, if you are so minded. This is what I have to say, these are my conditions. Now, what have you to say?"

The people were left without voice. Never had they imagined an utterance so shameless and so bold. They were as captives in the hands of an enemy.

Finally, Trailing Cloud found the words that must be said. "This is not for us to decide. We are but children who dwell here in the house of our fathers. Neither is it for you to decide, though you may beat us with clubs and drive arrows through us. But we will find the Holy One, and pass on your words to him."

He turned his back on the man on the roof and in his customary soft voice he said to the people: "I think we have already stayed too long. Take up the burden of our dead one. We must shelter her."

As the people moved away, they could not hear Dark Dealer's wrathful tones as he turned to his followers: "Where is that old goat-leaping fool? I counted on him to be leading those people. I counted on bargaining with him. We can't hold that water back forever—and once it breaks free, our advantage will be gone and we will have

to fight to hold what we now have." He paced rapidly
back and forth across the narrow roof space and as he
crossed in front of the fire, his body, which was not that
of a giant, threw the shadow of a giant across the roof of
the cavern.

"Some of you will have to slip out there, among those
people, and try to find that old goat. He can't be far away.
I advise you," he stopped, and his lips pulled back from
his teeth, "to be careful. You are Spider Clan men, and if
you are discovered out there your bodies will wind up at
the bottom of the canyon."

Chapter 13

Let Him Live—Despised

SALT realized that his name had been whispered over
and over again. At first it formed part of a frightening dream. He was being pursued in the flat
country above the canyon, and as he ran seeking shelter,
trees and rocks eluded him, disappearing into the air just
as he reached them, leaving him no choice but to run on,
while his lungs burst and his legs turned lifeless, and all
the while the pursuing voice called, "Salt! Salt! Wait for
my arrow! I am aiming between your shoulders! Just wait!
Salt! Salt!"

151

He escaped the dream at last. When he opened his eyes it was to find himself in darkness, his head throbbing with pain. He remained motionless, searching the darkness with his eyes.

Again the voice called his name. So there had been a reality in the dream after all! When it came again, he knew it as the voice of Day Singer; it seemed to be right at his ear.

He inclined his head slightly, to indicate his wakefulness. Then he heard: "We are in the kiva of the Spider Clan. There are four guards. Don't move. Be quiet." A long silence followed, until Salt began to wonder once more whether he was awake or dreaming. He wanted to move his head and examine his surroundings, but checked the action. Then the voice again.

"I must speak only a few words at a time. Wait. Don't move."

Thus, through long aching minutes, Salt learned what had happened. Day Singer had regained consciousness while he was being carried out of the underground passage, but he had concealed the fact. Turtle must have come to at about the same time, and they had managed to let each other know that they were alive and awake.

He and Turtle had been unwise. They had discovered the dam being built in the underground passage, had realized the purpose of it, and then had let themselves be struck down from behind. They had also recognized that the men in the underground passage were all of the Spider Clan, though they had not seen Dark Dealer.

All this he told in sounds that almost eluded Salt, hardly more than a word or two at a time, and Salt strained at listening until he thought his nerves would crack.

Then Day Singer said: "My bonds are untied. My hands are free . . . I also untied Turtle's hands . . . We waited until you were awake . . . Now I am going to untie your hands . . . Be careful, two guards back of us—I can't see them . . . Listen carefully . . . Turtle and I will rush guards standing by kiva ladder . . . We will grab their clubs if we can . . . Do our best to overpower them . . . That will bring the other guards to help . . . When you see four guards piling on us . . . Jump up and crawl through the ventilator hole . . . Holy One has plan for you . . . It is important that you get away . . . You will find him above . . . Entrance to secret trail . . . He is waiting . . . Now I will slide down toward your hands . . . If the guard is not watching . . ."

Nothing further happened. Salt heard nothing, no movement, no further words. When this silence had continued for some time, he began to wonder if Day Singer had fainted. He had been badly hurt and must have lost a quantity of blood. Yet Salt dared not look, dared not move. The agony of waiting was now greater than ever, since his hopes had been raised by Day Singer's plan of action. He knew how to lie waiting for game and to endure blistering sun or biting wind; he had practiced that through many hours. But this was a new experience. He was now the hunted, and the hunter stood somewhere out of sight. He had no signs to go by; no bird song breaking off at mid-point; no bright-eyed squirrel watching from a tree limb. Here was nothing but an agony of nerve and muscle.

His hands were tied behind and the thong which bound them passed down to his feet, which were doubled backward and tied together. A second thong passed from his hands upward and was fastened in a slip knot around his neck. Thus he could move neither hands nor feet without tightening the thong around his neck.

When it seemed that he could wait no longer and must shift his head or his body, he felt a movement at his back; it was so slight, so almost imperceptible, that he thought he must be mistaken. It seemed impossible that knots in a leather thong could be untied without tugging and pulling. Day Singer must be exploring the knots and deciding how to attack them. What was his amazement, then, when he felt his hands fall apart and the thong fall slack around his throat!

Day Singer's whisper came again: "Don't move! . . . Your feet are still tied . . . Turtle is ready . . . I will count ten . . . It will be up to you . . . to reach Holy One . . ."

Then—feet pounded on the roof overhead. Before Day Singer could even start his count, men were pouring down the kiva ladder. Salt lost track of their number. They sounded like men released from duty. They spoke loudly, laughing, "It is over! Now we have done it!"

This meant nothing to Salt; probably it meant nothing to Day Singer or Turtle either. But what would happen here in the kiva?

The guards who had been somewhere in the shadow

back of Salt moved toward the group gathered at the bottom of the ladder. "What has happened? We had to stay on guard duty. Tell us!"

Many explanations followed; many voices spoke at once. Salt felt shame and anger. He realized that disaster had fallen upon the village. He even understood that Eldest Woman had been murdered. Dark Dealer and the Spider Clan had captured the village. And he could do nothing! Surely it was impossible to carry out Day Singer's plan. They must die here, with nothing accomplished.

Perhaps Day Singer's thoughts moved in the same direction. He must have seen the hopeless situation. But his conclusion was different. At that moment he rose and his piercing yell rattled around the circular room. He hurled himself at a guard.

Next moment he had a war club. Still yelling, he swung right and left. Men reeled away from him.

Turtle, tall and thin, was alive and amazingly swift. An instant later, he hit the second guard. He too now held a war club.

Salt leaped as Day Singer lunged forward, and fell flat. He had forgotten to untie his legs! His numbed fingers fumbled at the knot. He tried to break the thong. The seconds passed. Day Singer and Turtle could not stand up against so many men for long. They still shouted, taunting the men they fought. The kiva ladder went down. No reinforcements could get into the kiva, but neither could Day Singer or Turtle escape.

Salt finally hobbled across the room toward the ventilator shaft, praying that no one saw him. He squirmed into the opening. Pulling with his hands, he went quickly. He was about to crawl into the larger opening beyond the kiva wall, when the leather thong jerked tight around his neck! He had been discovered! Someone had grabbed it from the other end! He reached for the thong, jerked it mightily. It came loose in his hands. It had caught against the edge of a rock! He was free!

At that moment a body fell upon him in the darkness. A hot stinking breath closed upon him. He heard words: "Not so fast, whoever you are. No one leaves by this door."

As Salt felt hands at his throat, his unseen, foul-smelling adversary made a sound that was half-groan and half-belch. The hands relaxed and Salt heard a familiar voice.

"The Holy One thinks you will be a leader, so you had better live a while longer." It was Shield.

"How did you know—" Salt began.

"We will talk later," Shield answered. "Day Singer and Turtle can't last long. This will stop pursuit for a while—" He moved in the darkness and Salt knew he was dragging the dead guard and crowding him into the narrow ventilator shaft.

Salt had freed his feet and slipped the thong from his neck. Moments later, Shield leading, they crawled through the crack in the outer rock and moved sideways across the cliff.

The stars shone clear and the smell of the pine trees and damp coolness came up from the canyon. The silence of the night came like a roar of mighty voices.

* * * * *

Shield did not take the upward trail as Salt expected. Instead, he scrambled across the face of the cliff until he reached the village trail, then started down. Salt almost called out that he was expecting to meet the Holy One in the country above, but perhaps it was better to travel in silence. He followed Shield and said nothing.

Within a very few minutes they had reached the bottom, were hurrying toward the spring; then Salt understood. There, where the canyon ended in a great half-circle, scattered among the boulders and the tall spruce and pine trees, the people of the Village of the White Rocks had gathered. A fire had been built, and the flames, leaping upward, cast a dancing, wavering light high against the canyon walls. It also lighted the faces of the people. At the center of them all, Salt saw, wonderingly, their leader, Blue Evening Sky, he whom they called Holy One.

As Salt approached, a small, quick-moving woman drew away from the crowd and came to him first. She stopped when she was still a few feet away and a clear shining smile lighted her face. His mother, Becoming Day, took one step closer and touched his arm.

"You are well. I rejoice. Happiness be yours."

It was a pleasant voice, as Salt would always remember. He answered: "May you have happiness, my Mother. I walk in your beauty."

They looked once more at each other and saw that all was well. Then Salt stood before the Holy One.

The old man smiled, and an expression of mischief seemed to play about his eyes.

"Peace, boy. We hoped you would finish sooner with entertaining that man up there."

"May your days and nights be in peace, Grandfather. The entertainment was not to my liking. What of Day Singer and Turtle?"

"You ask a hard question, my son." The old man turned back to the broken boulder on which he had been seated.

Men piled fresh logs on the fire and a burst of fiery sparks flew upward into the night. Salt saw that the people had been eating . . . the pots of cooked food were standing away from the fire. Even as he noticed this, his mother came bearing a bowl in which dried meat and corn had been cooked together.

"Our grandfather is cunning. He had food stored in his rock house." As she murmured the words, she looked shyly at the Holy One.

"Sit, boy, and eat," the Village Chief ordered. "You ask a difficult question. Some of us went up there and will try to get to Day Singer and Turtle before they are beaten to death. Other men wait at the barricade, threatening to attack from that side. I want no attack, if it can be avoided. Women and children are in there . . . our people if not our clansmen. You see," he smiled mockingly, "I am now a warrior, planning battles; not a man of peace."

"I cannot understand all that happened." Salt found eating difficult. "When I saw Flute Man murdered, I knew something was wrong. Maybe I should have reported this to you and the rest would not have happened."

The old one waved his hand. "You would not have

found me. I was up there ahead of you. I saw Flute Man
and waited. When he came to the entrance, there he stayed,
and there you found him. You were frightened . . . but
you went on, and proved to all of us that you have a man's
courage.

"If a mistake was made, I made it." The village leader
showed that he was troubled. "A great anger rose in me
when I realized that Flute Man had discovered the trail.
I slew him, the first man I ever slew with my hands. In
the quiet after anger, I went away. So, you would not have
found me."

Clearly he was troubled. The firelight revealed a look
of sorrow on his face. He turned to the elder men nearby:
Shield, Trailing Cloud, Cloud Head, Between Feathers
. . . all the leaders of the six clans represented there.

Shield answered, "The failing was not in you, but in
that man up there. He turned loose the anger that is in
us all. Many feel that he must be destroyed before we can
have peaceful minds again."

The Holy One pulled himself straight. "When I
walked alone up there, I decided that it is better for Dark
Dealer to destroy himself. This he will do. This he is already doing. He told the people that he has the power to
stop the spring, or to let it flow. This, of course, is a lie. He
built a dam of rocks, hoping that it would hold the water
long enough for him to win the village. But water is strong
even stronger than Dark Dealer or any of us. It will break
the dam, and we will have our spring again. And thus,
Dark Dealer destroys himself, step by step. I say there is
no need to have his blood on our hands."

Salt saw that Trailing Cloud, the Sun Watcher, was
rising to his feet, trembling in his infirmity, but borne up
by resolution. Erect at last, the old man held up his hand:
"Holy One's decision is wise, and we will abide with it.
But our hearts are heavy with grief for Eldest Woman.
And Day Singer and Turtle . . . what of them? Will they
also come to us lifeless? And are we to live with this too?"

Salt put aside his bowl, the food gone cold. Here were
terrible questions.

The Holy One, turning to Trailing Cloud, spoke in a
strong voice that carried to all the people. "We have a
law among us which can demand that a man give his life
for taking the life of another. We have many laws, demanding penalties. It is not enough to have a law. We
still must decide whether to use the full force of the law,
or to use it only in part. A law by itself cannot cure a man;
that is for us to accomplish, if it can be accomplished. This
I ask you: If we take the life of Dark Dealer in return
for the lives he has taken, that will finish it. He will be no
more, but will pass beyond our reach. But what if we hold
him here, alive, where the minds and the tongues of men
can play upon him? Is it not a greater justice that he should
stay, despised, in the company of men? He will resist, he
will plot against us, he will harm us if he can. But a man
is not a rock, he is not beyond touch, and his flesh and his
spirit can be hurt. I say, let this man live among us,
despised. Let children spit in his footprints. Let women
turn their faces from him. Let men refuse to hear him in
the kiva councils. This is what he will come to. The young
men who follow him today, even they will despise him.

"If he is at bottom a coward, and I think he may be, his own flint knife will save us the dishonor of taking his blood. But if he has the substance of a man, he will in time come to us and ask to start again. I say, let him live among us, despised."

Salt felt his blood warm at the fire of this old man's wisdom. Shame and outrage could come to a people, but they could still save themselves so long as their leaders remained firm.

No one voiced objection to the words of the Holy One. The people began to consider other problems. Crane Woman expressed the concern which faced them all. Out of the shadows she faced the Village Chief. "Perhaps we will agree to let Dark Dealer live with us. But where will we live? He has taken our village, our houses, our food. Unless we are willing to battle him and throw him out of there, I see no place to invite him to share with us." Crane Woman often spoke boldly, in a strong voice, then became shy immediately afterward, as if she had said more than she intended. Having spoken out in this forthright manner, she ducked her head and retreated back into the shadows.

The Village Chief was not embarrassed by such bold questioning. He thanked Crane Woman for speaking. Then he explained his plan. "We have not forgotten how to build houses, so let us build for our needs, here where we stand tonight. Stone and timber are here in abundance. Our spring will be restored and we will have water. We will keep a guard in the trail to prevent Dark Dealer from interfering with our water again. I think we will not have to remain here long. When Dark Dealer took our village, he forgot that he has only one clan on his side. We are six clans. We have ten men for every man of his, and the fields are in our possession. Our guard in the trail will prevent his people from going out to their farms. When he has eaten the food in our storehouses up there, he will realize his mistake. I think he will realize it long before the food is gone. As for ourselves, we will live well. Our crops will soon be ripe, and while we wait for them to ripen, our men will prove that they are still good hunters. Is this not enough? Will we not survive, my children?"

Probably no one would have dissented. Their leader, who this night had put aside the masquerade of wild talk and goatish capers, had thought out their problems for them. His plan was good, they would survive. Probably no questions would have been asked, but as it turned out, there was no opportunity that night for any further discussion.

The people heard first a rumble, as of thunder muttering in the distant mountains. Then it grew louder at once. It came closer. Then it was upon them with a shattering roar. People who had turned to listen, suddenly leaped to their feet and were terrified. They looked here and there but could not locate the source of the fearful cascading sound.

Then a shout went up! "The water! Our father, the spring!"

It was true. Water in great rolling muddy waves shot out of the rock at the bottom of the canyon, splashing high against obstructing boulders, sweeping along with a thunder of stones. The dam built by Dark Dealer had burst! The water would run in a mad flood until it had drained the underground lake.

Now people ran madly, crying their joy, to meet the rushing water. In the roar of the water their fears were drowned and washed away.

Only the Holy One failed to move, and Salt, of course, since he had been stopped by a gesture of the old man.

"They will not worry now. They will be content to build a new village, if necessary, and go on living as they always have. I think Dark Dealer will not hold out too long, and the people can move back into their homes.

"But what has happened will not be mended tonight, or tomorrow, or ever. You, my son, have lived to see the end of the life which our fathers lived before us. I have watched it coming a long time. Dark Dealer was not created from nothing, like a poisonous mushroom that seems to come from nowhere. Such a man is born only when the time and place are ready for him. The shell in which we lived is broken and may never be put together again. I told you, when last we talked, that you might be the one to save us. I want you to go on a journey, a long and dangerous journey, from which you may never return."

Now. It had come. Salt felt his scalp move and the muscles across his belly tighten. He remembered the moment underground, when he thought to perish in darkness. And he sensed that in this new venture, such moments of uncertainty and fear would occur again and again.

"My Grandfather," he said slowly, pondering his words,

"am I the one to do this? Have I the courage? Can I endure?"

In the darkness he did not observe that the older man smiled. "You have learned something in three days. When we talked before, you had not yet been frightened. Yes, you are the one to go. We have no other to send. Those of us who have the experience for such a journey have not the strength. Others, who might be stronger, have not your desire to help your people. I am only sorry that you must go at once; better if you could train for this journey, but we have no choice. We will survive what Dark Dealer has done, but our life here is broken and will never be put together again in the way it was before. We must find a new way, and I have no knowledge of what that will be."

"But how am I to do this?" The venture, alone, with no hand upon his shoulder, became suddenly real. Salt saw himself failing, and his people with him. His heart seemed to die. Weakly he asked: "How will I know what to bring back to our people?"

Silence followed, a long silence. The fire had died, the men who had been feeding logs to it had all rushed off to watch the spouting water. As the fire died, night flowed back into the canyon. Out of that night, Holy One spoke at last.

"I cannot tell you what to look for, or what to bring back. That is the terrible thing about this journey of yours. I can only tell you that somewhere in the south lies a land our fathers called the Land of Fable. We know nothing about it, but we are told that our songs, our dances, and our Mother Corn came from there.

"One day we talked about the corn you planted down here in the canyon. What I didn't tell you then is something I heard my father talk about, and something I have watched myself. A field of corn is like a village of people —so my father would say. If people stay too long among themselves, they weaken themselves, some families die out entirely. He encouraged young men from other villages to come among us, marry our girls, and become part of us. He also encouraged our men to go elsewhere to find wives. On your journey south, you will find some of our people.

"A race of corn will become weak in the same way. No man among us can say how long we have had our corn. It has been too long. Water will make the stalks grow tall, as you discovered by planting down here. But we looked at your corn—and while the ears are not fully formed, they will be no thicker and no longer than the ears of the plants in the dry land above. I have watched this since my father's time, and I now understand what he talked about.

"Is it a new race of corn that is needed, then? I cannot say. Maybe what is needed is that our people should change. We are no longer the children we were when our songs, our dances, and our Mother Corn first came among us. We cannot live in fullness with these things as once we did. We try to reach beyond them.

"So, whether it is corn, or people, at fault, I cannot say. I have helped as much as I can. The rest is up to you.

"I cannot even say whether I will be here when you return. But if you are successful, our people will honor you. You will be their leader, and you will make their

lives whole again. I think that what you must look for will
be something that comes from our Father the Sun. It will
live in him. It will lift up our hearts.

"And now, my son, I give you this turquoise stone from
my own neck. It is as a part of my body; it will keep you
secure against all enemies; it will hold up your heart
when you are troubled."

The giving of the turquoise, there in the darkness, was
the most shattering experience of all that long day. Salt
felt as if the image in which he had been born had been
broken, and he had been born a new person.

"We will talk again tomorrow," the Holy One was
saying. "There will be much to discuss, many things that
you must carry in your mind as you journey from us."

Chapter 14

Southward

THE EAGLE spread its wings and plunged free of the brown crag. It drifted downward, following the high slope of the barren mountain, then caught the hot-air currents rising from the valley and let itself be swept higher and higher until it seemed to pass beyond the empty sky.

The man-creature moved alone, like a mole blindly groping. Twice the hard-eyed eagle circled the broad valley, watching.

The sands of a dried-up stream bed gleamed white as bone. A chain of low rounded hills showed red scars where wind and water had cut through the surface of grass and soil. The eagle tilted downward, descended rapidly out of the blue, leveled and circled. It flew up to the end of the long valley, skirted the apron of the high mountains in the north, wheeled and, descending still lower, hovered in space.

When the man-creature still moved, the great bird pumped its wings and sailed away.

Salt had come down out of the mountains, out of the timbered coolness and the tumbling streams, and journeyed now in low hot country. It was only midmorning, but the sun burned with an intensity he had never before experienced. He would not walk much farther into the heat of the day, only as far as the low-lying hills before him, where a pocket of dark green promised water. He saw the circling eagle, watched it soar westward up the long running valley and return. But the boy was not dismayed. The heat was great, but not unbearable; he felt strong, tireless. He was embarked on a journey which no other man in his village had been asked to make. The eagle did not worry him.

It was important to go swiftly, yet it was also important to reach his goal. He must not try too much in one day, for what he gained in overexertion he would lose afterward in resting. He trotted, then walked, then rested. Trotted, walked, rested. He had no way of telling time, but he tried to keep to the same time intervals in trotting and walking, and to rest lying flat on his back only long enough to get his breath and give his leg muscles time to relax.

Walking alone, he thought of the things he had been told by the Village Chief, by his mother, and by others at leave-taking: the world in which he moved was less strange and less empty when he kept his mind on such things.

The Village Chief—they would always call him the Holy One, even though he had left the rock shelter, talked straight, and was leader of his people again—had not said much. "You will be gone a long time . . . you will cover great distances . . . you will not remember too many things. Besides, I do not know the road you are taking and I cannot tell you all that you will meet."

The Chief was concerned that the boy conduct himself properly. "Be friendly," he told him. "If you show no fear of strangers, they will respect you. They may help you."

Salt thought of these words, as he trotted, walked and rested. He thought about them against the background of his knowledge of people. If he met a stranger who was unafraid, would he be friendly? Helpful? He could answer for himself, but he did not know about others. Some men would be rude to strangers, as they were rude to anyone else. Perhaps if you took no notice of rudeness and continued being friendly, it would work. He would remember the advice.

The Chief also said: "Be watchful. You will be in strange country and none of us can tell you which turn to take, what river to follow, how to cross a mountain which may lie before you. Only remember that you will be

traveling south all the time. You must have the sun on
your left when you start in the morning. You must have
it on your right when you stop at night. If you must go
around a mountain, take the side that will lead you soonest
south. When you cross a stream, look for the place where
the current breaks into many ripples, for there it will be
shallow and you will have rock underfoot. Watch everything as you go."

When Salt reached the low-lying hills and sought out
the pocket of green, he found no live stream, but the
water oozed to the surface in shallow pools. He also found
sharp hoofprints and knew that an occasional deer stopped
to drink. With a pointed rock, he dug out one of these
pools and made a trench leading away from it. This would
drain off the stagnant water and let fresh water enter.
Then he lay down to rest in the shade of tall mesquite trees.

He had been told that when he came down out of the
mountains he would find a river flowing from the east,
and following downstream, he would find a second river
coming up from the south. It was important to find this
second stream, because living near it were friendly people
who could tell him about the road southward.

He thought about this as he lay resting. The season had
matured into full summer; ripened corn and beans were
being gathered in all the fields he passed. He had not
realized, setting out, how many people, how many villages,
lay beyond the Village of the White Rocks. He even met
people who spoke his own language, and this too surprised
him. When these strangers found they could talk to him,
they asked where he came from, what house or clan he

belonged to, and they wondered where he was going. In offering food, they suggested that he might not find food where he was going, or he might not find friendly people. To all these invitations to discuss his journey, Salt only thanked them for their kindness and remarked that he had a long way to go and must not delay. All were friendly, even those who did not speak his language. None tried to detain him.

Of the people who lived on the stream flowing from the south, some were men and women from his own village. The Holy One spoke of them. They had married down there and no longer belonged to the north. But they would speak his language and would help him.

He rested until the greatest heat had gone out of the day, then climbed to the top of the low hill and looked across the wide valley for a landmark. Heat ran fluidly across the horizon and a distant purple mountain seemed to hang, without foundation, from the sky.

When he left the low-lying hill and started down through the desert's thorny brush and cactus, a gray wolf jumped from a ledge of rock on a neighboring hill and followed cautiously after him.

He camped that night without water, but at least he had the flesh of a rabbit to roast. His camp was in a dry arroyo where a fire could be built without arousing curiosity.

Salt's traveling equipment was simple. To get food, he carried a curved rabbit stick, a sling, a flint knife, and a long net made of fine brown cotton thread. On his feet he wore moccasins, the soles of heavy rawhide; an extra pair hung from his belt. A pouch of dried corn and a second pouch of dried meat constituted his reserve food supply, and a small pitch-covered basket carried water. His breech-clout was a long piece of white cotton material doubled over his belt at front and back with the ends hanging to his knees. A sleeveless jacket hung from a thong that crossed over one shoulder and under the opposite arm.

On the fourth day after coming down from the mountains, Salt found the river and the people dwelling there, a country of willows and great crowned cottonwood trees. Their houses, stretching for miles along the river, filled him with wonder. They were simple houses, flat-roofed, made of poles and intertwined willow saplings covered with adobe mud. Inside, even in the great heat of midday, these dwellings were dim and cool. Before each house rose a shaded shelter of poles covered with brush. Here in coolness the people cooked their meals, told their stories, and slept at night.

What astonished Salt were the irrigated fields. The people built dams of brush and stone at many places along the river and trenched canals that carried water far out into the flat valley. Looking at these canals for the first time, he was both joyful and sad . . . joyful to behold so much water, but sad that his own people did not share it.

Salt found the people from his village and was made welcome, as if he had been a younger brother. He must stay to be feasted. Indeed, he was feasted by each of the headmen in turn. The time was not lost, they assured him, when they heard of his plans for journeying south; and when they told him of the great summer rains which turned shallow desert rivers into whirling torrents that flooded entire valleys, he was content to stay. So he waited in that pleasant land, feasted, and heard stories of the people he would meet and the things he would see.

Even as he enjoyed himself, however, Salt examined the corn that he ate, and was disappointed to find that it was identical with the corn his people grew at home. Then he would recall those who waited for him . . . he would wonder if the new houses were built, if his people had food. Then becoming restless, he begged to be allowed to resume his journey.

In the end, the leader of the clan insisted on sending his own son, River Fighter, to accompany Salt as far as certain kinsmen living many days' journey to the south.

When Salt left that land of water, planted fields and crowned cottonwood trees, the fierce heat of summer had passed. The people, having become fond of him, uttered last words of advice, of what he should do, how to conduct himself, even words of regret. They gave him thick-soled sandals woven of tough yucca fibers and would have loaded him down with food and gifts if he had not protested that he was too frail for their bounty.

As he took to the trail, his heart sang as on a morning in spring. River Fighter was almost his own age and, like his tribesmen, was burned quite dark by the southern sun. He was handsome, good-natured, full of laughter, a happy traveling companion.

They set forth at dawn and followed the shallow valley of the northward-flowing river. They passed between the shadows of low, boulder-strewn mountains into a seemingly endless valley that opened before them. After many days they reached a height of land from which, henceforth, all streams would flow southward; all streams would carry Salt farther and farther into the Land of Fable, the Red Land of the South.

Soon they picked up the headwaters of one of these southward-flowing streams and on a morning when the desert doves talked and the rising sun stood in golden haze, Salt and his companion said farewell and Salt went on alone.

Distances were great, but it was not a lonely land. Hardly a day passed when he did not see a cluster of mud-roofed houses. Sometimes the clusters were large enough to be called a village, stretching along the banks of a swift stream pouring from a mountainside; sometimes only a few lonely dwellings scattered at the edge of a cornfield.

The land, except in rocky stretches and in flats where the earth glistened white with alkali, was everywhere clothed in fierce tangles of scrubby brush and branched cactus trees that stood above the scrub like silent men watching children at play. When he came to these thickets, he watched carefully to distinguish between game trails and the paths of men. The game trails might lead only to a water hole or a feeding ground, but man-trails would lead him on his way. Often he had to backtrack for hours before he found the road he wanted.

It was not a lonely land. The farther south he traveled, the more thickly populated he found it. Even when he encountered no man or woman, he knew that people were nearby. Everywhere along the trail, he found wayside shrines. These might appear to be no more than a heap of rocks piled at the trailside, with bright-colored feathers attached to protruding sticks. But he never failed to take up a rock from the roadside, breathe upon it, and, as taught him in childhood, lay it atop the pile. This in courtesy to the Cloud People.

This practice, unwittingly on his part, had several times saved his life. Men of strange tribes had followed him, distrusting him as they distrusted any stranger. Trailing him silently, as a wolf or a puma might have trailed him, they saw him perform his act of grace; thereafter he went on unmolested.

It was not a lonely land.

Day followed day. Days of hunger. Days of thirst. Days when insects swarmed about him, stinging and biting. Days of longing for his people, for the look of searching tenderness of his mother, for the kindly speech of the Holy One. Days of fever and quick, shuddering chills, when the food he ate was vomited up again and his legs seemed ready to break under the effort of walking.

At last the houses as well as the people were new and strange. The dwellings were circular with dome-shaped roofs. Long slender poles were bent into arches, tied at the top, and roofed with mats woven from palm leaves. Clusters of these houses, with their shaded outdoor living places, were found in clearings, a stream running by. It was surprising to see men from these villages trotting ahead of him down a trail, with quarters of a deer or other burden suspended from each end of a pole carried across the shoulders. It was a thing to remember and to tell about when he returned home . . . if he ever returned.

The excitement of new things passed, but weariness remained. If Salt could have seen himself, he would hardly have recognized his own image. His ribs, the bones at his elbows, shoulders, hips and knees showed through the thin flesh. Arms and legs were gashed by many thorns, some of them poisonous, causing his flesh to swell and mortify. Such wounds were slow in healing. His body was often mud-spattered, his long hair matted and unkempt.

He crossed some five or six large rivers and numerous branch streams—he tried to keep count of the rivers, for he knew that after a certain number he would come to one which he must follow inland, away from the sea—but in time the many crossings blurred together and he lost count.

Finally he stood upon a low foothill that extended like an arm out of the mountains to the east, and he looked down into a broad flood-plain at his feet. He had come upon a world still different from any he had ever known.

The land had continued to change, growing warmer, damper, more densely forested. Now, impenetrable jungles ranged before him. Vines and creepers twined themselves around all growth, lashing it together. But the trail was now a broad avenue leading southward . . . at times a kind of tunnel through a green underworld. The pounding feet of many generations of men had kept it clear of growth, its direction certain. Here, trade and communication flourished.

It was more than the countryside that had altered. Looking down in astonishment upon the flood-plain, he saw a community of houses exceeding in number anything he had ever imagined. In the broad valley it seemed as if dwellings extended all the way to the horizon; not scattered aimlessly across the valley, but divided into planned sections, with roads between. The houses were of mud, fashioned in square blocks like the stones of which his own village was built, the roofs a thick covering of long bleached grass. Here and there among the houses, on low man-built earth hills, large buildings had been erected. Salt recognized these as holy places.

His wonder increased when, descending, he followed a road wide enough for ten men to walk abreast, and came at last among the houses. People gazed upon him curiously, but unlike the villagers whom he had met back in the mountains, they made no effort to stop him or talk to him. They were taller than any people he knew, and they dressed in bright colors. The women wore an upper garment, loose at the neck, with wide, flowing sleeves, and a skirt reaching below the knees. Intertwined in their dark braided hair were bright ribbons and feathers of many colors. They wore necklaces and ear and arm ornaments of sparkling shells, pearls, turquoise, and little copper bells. Some men wore robes reaching from the shoulder almost to the ground, and some, whom he took to be warriors, wore headdresses with brilliant plumage flashing as they walked. These carried round shields covered with leather, on which curious designs were painted.

He came to an open place within the town where people crowded elbow to elbow. Around the four sides of this open place stood small booths in which were displayed a great wealth of foods, cooked and uncooked; goods woven of cotton, feathers, and strange fibers; ornaments of gold and shell; baskets; pottery of many curious designs; caged birds and small animals; carved objects of wood and stone —countless things he had never seen or imagined. Here was pottery that surpassed belief; of black and red with brown and cream lines and whirls; some with a fluting up and down the sides; and so highly polished as to reflect his image. But what held his attention longest were small jars, dark brown, highly polished, and engraved with a sharp point in designs that suggested the delicacy of feathers. He stared a long time at this, and somehow felt here all the alien quality, the foreboding, the hidden dangers of this new world into which he had come.

As he lingered in the open place gazing about him, he was a strange figure. His sandals were frayed to shreds; his legs covered with scratches and angry sores; his body streaked with dust and mud; his hair matted. He seemed not to be aware of this, and the people who brushed past him seemed scarcely to look his way. But he was noticed.

He was accosted by two men bearing tall painted wooden staffs and wearing headdresses from which dangled eagle claws. They spoke to him in an unknown tongue; but when they touched his elbows, one on each side, and motioned to a large flat-roofed building facing the open square, he knew that he was to go with them.

But for what purpose? Instinctively, his hand sought the protecting turquoise at his neck.

Chapter 15

Still Southward

SALT was led through an open doorway into a courtyard, in the center of which lay a pool, green with
lily pads. Doorways opened upon this courtyard
from the rooms surrounding it on all sides.

The men walking on either side led him past the pool,
which he would have stopped to admire if he had been
alone. A fingerling fish flashed silver at him from the
shadows beneath the lilies. When his escorts reached the
open doorway opposite the street entrance, one went
ahead into the room, while the second, after motioning to
Salt to proceed, followed in the rear.

They entered a long narrow room, and, though the walls were whitewashed, Salt coming from bright sunlight found it dark. Several moments passed before he discerned three men seated at a table at the far end of the room. Silently they observed this stranger, then the middle one spoke sharply. He was answered by one of the escorts. Salt then realized that the man behind the table was speaking to him. The man spoke again, repeating his words, each time in a louder voice.

"I am Salt," said the boy proudly. "My people live there, in the north," he gestured northward.

The men all stared at him, then at each other. His speech was as strange to them as theirs to him.

The trio at the table spoke among themselves, pointing several times at Salt. It seemed they were more interested in the turquoise at his neck than in him. One of his guards approached closely and examined the stone. Presently the center man at the table clapped his hands. He seemed to give orders to one of the guards, who went out.

Again the men at the table talked among themselves, while Salt, trying to assure himself that their voices were friendly, began to feel uneasy. He tried again to explain himself, pointing to the north and to the south, but they only regarded him coldly.

In a little while the messenger returned and was followed by five other people, one an elderly woman. More talk, more pointing at Salt. One by one, the newcomers stepped forward and addressed Salt, each in a different language. So the men were seeking an interpreter.

The last to try was the woman. She wore the shoulder

mantle and the knee-length skirt customary with those people, and her hair in two braids tied together at the back. In her small round face her quiet eyes studied him before she spoke. This time the attempt was successful; it was reassuring to hear words in his own tongue even though pronounced haltingly, and with a strange accent. The three men, she told him, one a judge-priest and the other two his assistants, suspected him of being a spy, from a tribe north across the river. This city, she told him, was called Culiacan; its inhabitants were as numberless as the pines on the mountain, and they were suspicious of strangers among them. Then she asked why he wore a turquoise stone.

He understood that he was in danger. He must choose his words with care, must make the woman understand. He told her of the Village of the White Rocks; that his people were poor, but were men of peace who never made war or sent out spies. He had come this long journey seeking help. With many gestures he explained that the turquoise stood for the sky, where the sun lived; that it also stood for peace and long life, and it was the badge of his Turquoise Clan. He added, "Whoever wears the turquoise, travels in the protection of the gods." When he had finished, he looked for understanding in the woman's face.

While he watched in growing anxiety she explained at length to the three men who listened, eying him thoughtfully. Again they consulted among themselves. Then the one in the center, the judge-priest, rose from the wooden bench. As his cape of a pale-blue material fell back Salt saw, on his bare chest, a large disk in which turquoise, obsidian, white shell and some kind of pink stone were inlaid in an intricate mosaic.

He spoke first to the woman, quietly; then turning to Salt's guards his tone grew more peremptory. They left the room.

The woman, touching Salt's arm, said: "You come."

Salt, puzzled, looked to the men behind the table. Their gesture seemed to dismiss him.

In the street, the woman repeated, "You come."

She took him to her house, a few doors away, where were her two young daughters and an older boy. She gave orders, and the children brought cook pots, blew life into the fire in the outdoors cooking place, and fetched articles of clothing. That was like his mother. In a daze he stood watching the activity until the woman pushed him into an enclosed yard. He recognized the pot of yucca suds which the two daughters had just prepared. Presently he was kneeling while the woman washed his hair. This too was like being home again. Surely he was now safe with these people.

Meanwhile, the son of the household prepared the sweat bath which stood in the corner of the walled yard. When this was ready, the woman and her daughters retired. Salt went in to steam, and to wash himself afterward with water dipped in a gourd ladle from a large pottery jar. The son helped in this, smiling, and afterward showed Salt how to array himself in the new and curious garb of these people. The breechclout, a long strip of soft woven material, was passed between the legs, wrapped twice around the body, and the loose ends, tucked under and over at front and back, hung to the knees. New sandals made with a stiff leather sole; a robe of white cloth, on which a border of geometrical figures was embroidered in many colors, completed the costume.

When Salt returned to the house the woman was waiting, smiling a vague welcome. Then he saw waiting the two men who had led him before the judge-priest. His feeling of well-being died within him. So it had not been dismissal; some further ordeal awaited him.

But the woman must have guessed his emotion; her smile quickened reassuringly.

"You go to feast at priest's house," she said. "These people have Turquoise Clan, like you people. The priest belong that clan. Good fortune for you." And clapped her hands together, like a child who takes delight in a trick.

Salt could only ask, "What is your name? What may I call you?"

"They call me Yucca Flower Woman."

That night Salt ate strange foods from the sea, meats like no other he knew, and fruits beyond any dream. Many sat at the table, their faces gleaming in torchlight, Salt among them. From a ragged stranger looked upon with distrust, he had been transformed into an honored guest. The Holy One had spoken with truth when he said of the turquoise, "It will keep you secure."

So Salt went on from Culiacan. In the weeks that followed, he traveled through a country of marshes and lagoons, where sea birds wheeled and screamed. Villages built on broad earthen mounds above the surrounding land.

Then the trail turned away from salt water and the marsh-
lands and followed a river that clove the mountains lying
to the east. Now he had reached the last stage of his
journey. The Land of Fable lay somewhere beyond the
mountains which, as he traveled eastward in suffocating
jungle heat, arose in great blue ridges that seemed to climb
into the sky itself.

He was troubled now by a new concern. Culiacan had
taught him that without knowledge of the language of the
people he was to meet, he could never explain his mission,
nor understand whatever they tried to tell him. Indeed,
for lack of their speech, he might be slain as an enemy spy.

Also, coming to the end of his journey, what was he to
bring back with him? Would it be an object that he could
carry in his hands? Would it be something he could observe, and carry back as a picture in his mind? Or something to hear, such as a ritual, a nine days' recitation of
songs? If it was the corn spoken of by the Holy One, how
could he know when he had found the right kind? He had
come a long and difficult journey, and the thought that he
might return home empty-handed filled him with anguish
for his people.

On many nights, as he lay down to sleep in desert arroyo
or leafy jungle, he saw the faces of the people in the Village of the White Rocks and wondered what had happened
to them. Was Dark Dealer still holding out in the village?
Had the new houses been built in the canyon? Who had
been ambushed? Murdered? Winter was now upon them,
and he wondered if the fields had yielded enough to feed
the people through the bleak months. And what of his

mother and his young sister? These were heavy thoughts to carry up a mountain trail. Unlike a burden strapped to one's back, they could not be put down for a resting period.

Finally, he was out of the suffocating heat of the coast jungle and journeying in the highlands where pine trees flashed their red trunks and fir and spruce brought a smell of home. He crossed the main range of the west and began to pass from one broad mountain valley to another. The villages increased in size again, the valley lands were richly tilled. He saw houses of stone, temples reared against the sky.

The trail had become a busy highway. Each day he encountered travelers. Sometimes he would pass a long file of villagers, each of whom would glance up, touch hand to forehead, then pass on, making no attempt to stop or to talk. At other times, hearing voices in speech or in song behind him, he would step off the trail and watch a file of men and women come trotting along, the men burdened with great piles of pottery ware, baskets, fibers for weaving, animal hides, while the women carried the burden of a child slung in a shawl at their backs. They too would touch hand to forehead as they passed Salt at the roadside, and resume a song broken off.

One afternoon he approached a large lake that spread its blue waters between mountain headlands. As he neared, a flight of ducks passed overhead, circled, and came to light close to the lake shore. He was hungry; duck flesh, after a steady diet of rabbit, squirrel and dried deer meat would be delicious. He hurried to the lake's edge, grabbing up small stones for his sling, and seeking a hiding place among the reeds. At the water's edge he crouched, waiting. The ducks should soon swim within range.

After a moment he noticed a number of large gourds floating on the water close to shore. The ducks were swimming around these gourds, diving into the shallow bottom, and discussing the things that ducks talk about among themselves. A light warm breeze blew off the lake, pushing ahead small shallow waves to splash upon the shore. The floating gourds bobbed up and down in the restless water, but moved no closer inland.

And even stranger, one of the gourds was floating away from its fellows, toward the place where the ducks were thickest. In amazement, he saw a duck disappear from the surface of the water, not in a dive, but seeming to plunge down all at once. A streak of red appeared on the surface of the water and spread in a circle.

Immediately a second duck disappeared beneath the surface; again that streak of red. Surely some strange animal had got among the ducks and was destroying them.

Salt rose then, fitted a stone to his sling, swung it around his head. It flew like a speeding arrow. The stone cracked squarely in the center of the floating gourd.

The gourd seemed to explode. A pair of eyes, human eyes, gazed at him through the fragments of the gourd shell.

The ducks rose in wild clamor, their wings whistling as they took to the air in panic. The person in the water moved a few feet toward shore, then slowly emerged.

Salt stared in amazement at the man standing half submerged. He shook off the fragments of gourd shell and two ducks dangled from his belt. Their heads had been twisted off under water.

It was an awkward moment. Salt knew he must act quickly. He raised his hand, palm forward, moving it back and forth. Among the people in the north, this was a sign for negation. It could mean "no," "nothing," "no more." Then he made the gesture for eating, moving his index finger forward toward his mouth, and pointing in the direction taken by the flight of ducks.

After that, he could only wait. The man in the water continued to stare, then waded ashore. This stranger, while not much older than himself, was taller, and probably more powerful in combat. He wore a knife in his belt.

The stranger spoke at last, in speech unknown to Salt.

Salt smiled, answering in his own tongue: "In the north, a stranger is a friend until he shows himself to be otherwise. I hope your people have the same custom." He smiled again, to show his friendly intentions.

The stranger spoke again, jerked his chin toward a spot farther down the lake shore, and moved in that direction. Salt followed him, happily interpreting this as an invitation.

Around a low head of land a canoe was drawn up on the beach. The boy dropped his two ducks in the bottom of the canoe and motioned Salt to take a place in the bow. The canoe, hollowed out of a cedar log, was long and narrow, and the paddle a round piece of cedarwood fastened with thongs to a slender pole. They shoved off from shore.

On impulse, Salt patted the side of the craft and asked

how it was named. He repeated the gesture several times, saying, "What do you call this? How is it said?"

The canoeman, facing Salt from the stern, puzzled over Salt's words. Then his face cleared. He freed his right hand from the paddle, patted the side of the canoe and gave the word "icharuta."

Salt repeated the word "icharuta, icharuta." Then he pointed to some fish in the bottom of the boat and repeated his question, "How is it said?"

The answer came at once, "Akumara."

The strangeness between them seemed to disappear, and Salt decided that whoever this young man was, whatever his family might be, he would remain long enough to learn the language.

Spring came gently in that land. The oak forests on the hillside turned from brown to green in a matter of days. The heavy winter rains slacked off and after a few days of steaming, the earth appeared fresh-washed and bright with new color. Almost immediately, the warmth of summer descended.

Salt, in these months, became a member of a family—the family of the duck hunter, whose name Salt soon learned meant the ocelot, the wildcat of this region. Bringing Salt home that first day, he told of the meeting at the lake as a joke on himself. It produced laughter in the family and Salt was accepted almost at once. They made him display his slingshot and later he demonstrated his marksmanship with it.

Ocelot's family lived in a whitewashed adobe house, one

of many houses facing on a long street that curved with the shore of the blue lake, Patzcuaro. The house roofs were of thatch and sloped in four directions from a high ridge.

The father belonged to the family of the calzonci, the ruling chief of the area. As a member of that family, he was an official of the state and had charge of the fields which each year produced revenue for the state's upkeep. In the household were the grandfather and grandmother, who kept themselves busy; Ocelot's married sister, with her husband and two small children; and two younger brothers, who ate the morning and evening meal with the family, but in between times, as they said, practiced at being hunters and warriors. They accepted Salt as their instructor in the use of the slingshot and the rabbit stick.

Salt was awed by Ocelot's mother, since he had never before known a woman who did not grind her own corn, cook her own meals, and plaster her own house. Women and girls from nearby houses came each day to grind corn on the stone metate, an older woman prepared the family meals, and still another woman went each morning to the market in the center of the city and obtained the day's food. The mother, whose name meant Flowering Shaft of the Yucca, walked in the garden which swept down a long hill, bordered by an adobe wall, where birds of many plumages lived in reed cages, and a tame deer came to feed from her hand.

This city beside the lake seemed a place of wonder. In Salt's country, each man tilled his own field, hunted for his own meat, obtained his own firewood, held office in

clan or village, and had his own place in the ceremonies
of the people; but here a man did but one thing and had
to depend upon others for those needs which he could not
supply himself. Some men were carpenters, others were
stonemasons, and some even devoted their whole time to
building and repairing temples. Among the most highly
regarded of all craftsmen were the men who worked in
gold, silver, and precious stones.

Religious ceremonies were occasions involving large
masses of people and solemn spectacles. The temples, built
high on a squared-off pyramid, stood out in bold relief
against the sky. Great fires were built before these temples and the people moved in slow processionals, clothed
in bright costumes, chanting through the days and nights.

By spring Salt could speak the new language well enough
to explain what had happened to his people and why he
had come on this journey. When he turned to Ocelot's
father, however, and asked for help and advice, he was
not encouraged. The old man either frowned and walked
away, or refused to continue the discussion.

But one day he said suddenly, "It is the Valley of
Mexico of which you speak. A sorry land it is. Once the
gods smiled upon it, and in gratitude the people built
temples, cities of stone. If you go, you will see all these,
but you will see them in ruins. Jaguars come out of the
hills and walk the ruined streets. Thieves and murderers
too roam the streets. What was once great is so no more.
I would not urge you to go there. A slashed throat may
be all you will find."

But Salt refused to be discouraged. The Mother Corn

of his people had come from this far land, what Ocelot's father called the Valley of Mexico. Now that the Land of Fable bore a name, it became a place in reality, no longer a legend. In such a place he would find people, and the people would help him. This he believed, as the young will always believe.

Salt poured out his hopes to Ocelot. They talked together into the night; and Ocelot, obedient son though he was, was finally captured by the excitement of Salt's quest.

His decision to accompany Salt was, after some hesitancy, reported to his father. His father stifled his anger; fathers, in that land, trained their sons to be independent of spirit, as well as obedient, so now Ocelot's parent acknowledged within himself that the son had the right to come to his own decision, however foolish it might appear to be.

"If you must go, I won't prevent it," the elder said, not wholly hiding his displeasure. More calmly, he continued: "I will give you the name of a friend in that land; if he has not been murdered, he will be an old man now. He is master over a large household; his clansmen will still acknowledge his leadership. See him; he will help if he can."

It was a strange farewell, offering little comfort, and no blessing.

Within a few days Salt and Ocelot left the city on the lake and traveled eastward.

Chapter 16

Houses in the Sky

S ALT knew that at last he had come to the end of his
journey. During the last days of travel with Ocelot,
they passed greater and greater numbers of people
on the broad road. Here were buildings of stone, larger
buildings, before which stood great carved pillars. The
towns grew larger, and in the center of each was a high
pyramid standing above the surrounding buildings, surmounted by a temple and often a curl of smoke rising from
a sacrificial fire.

As they walked along, Salt expressed his amazement at
these sights, and at each outburst his companion would
voice a different view. If Salt remarked on the crowds of

people they were passing, Ocelot pointed out that quite as many people came to the market in his town. If Salt bent his head backward to gaze at a temple standing against the hot blue sky, Ocelot commented: "We have just such temples. You saw them in the middle of Tzintzuntzan, our town."

They were too good friends to argue, but Salt would smile. Maybe the crowds only seemed larger, the buildings and temples more beautiful, because he expected them to be. This was what he had been sent to find, in this land of great expectation!

He and Ocelot had come to be as close as brothers since that day on the lake, when Salt had proved his skill with a sling. In spite of his slight advantage in age, Ocelot was content to follow behind the purposeful boy from the north.

When at last they mounted the last ridge lying to the west and started down in the valley where lay the lakes and their girdle of cities, no doubt or question remained. Even Ocelot stood and looked wonderingly. Mist hung low above lake water and spread out over the neighboring land, where it was pierced by rows of cypress spires. Pine-covered islands and headlands floated upon this mist. Nearer at hand, where the sun plunged into the mist and gave it liveliness, a pyramid and its surmounting temple, sparkling in morning light, seemed to be of the sky, not of the earth.

The young travelers looked long at the view below them, then at each other, and neither uttered a word. This truly was the Land of Fable.

Tenayuca was that first city. In the next days, following the marshy lake shore alive with birds, they passed through Azcapotzalco, Coyotlatelco, Tlacopan, Chapultepec and Coyoacan. From the latter town, a roadway extended across the entrance to Lake Xochimilco. The lake was shallow, and the roadway was built by driving logs into the mud in two rows and filling the space between with stones and dirt. An opening midway between the two shores, covered over by a bridge, allowed the water to circulate as the lake level rose and fell.

At last they came to Culhuacan, the end of the journey, where lived the friend of Ocelot's family.

Days later, when Salt had accustomed himself somewhat to the great strange house and the people in it, he thought back over the long journey and, for the first time, felt astonished at what he had accomplished. If he had known of the thirst and the hunger, the poisonous thorns, and the long empty spaces through which he had traveled, would he have dared to start? Would he have the courage to return when the time came? It seemed to him, now that he knew the perils, impossible.

Here in the pleasant security of Tula's house, the Village of the White Rocks was like a dream that begins to fade from memory. The moments of fear, anger, and high resolve once real, were becoming like parts of a tale he might have heard at some long-ago time. Difficult to feel that he himself had been involved. So he felt less need to act recklessly or with speed.

The house of Tula was built on northward sloping land. At the foot of the slope, stretching beyond the horizon to the north, the great Lake Texcoco lay speckled by the sun. Back of the house rose the cone-shaped Hill of the Star, surmounted by a temple whose white stone flashed sunrays as if it were itself a star.

This house of Tula was a house of peace and quiet. Its great courtyard was large enough to have included the entire Village of the White Rocks, Salt thought. Cypress and pine ran in rows across the lower end where, catching the prevailing wind, they made a pleasant murmur. A covered walk ran along the four sides of the courtyard, shading the rooms which opened on it.

An arched gate led to a garden on the east, enclosed within a fence of living cactus. This gateway also led into a smaller courtyard beyond the main building, where the women had their quarters along with the cooking fires and baking ovens. At the head of the courtyard was the council room where Tula's clansmen met.

After his first meeting with the master of the house, which occurred late one afternoon, Salt had no occasion to meet and talk with Tula again for many days, though he was sometimes present, silent and preoccupied, at the evening meal.

The first person in the household with whom Salt became acquainted was the slave girl who came each morning bearing a lacquered tray, on which were a cup of hot chocolate and a rolled tortilla pierced with a cactus thorn. She never looked up, but after placing the tray on a low bench backed away, her eyes downcast.

At first Salt assumed that she was a younger daughter of the family, until Ocelot explained that women of the

family stayed within their own quarters. Only a slave girl
was allowed to serve strangers.

Even when he talked to her, Salt could not get the girl
to look up. She came each morning, placed the chocolate
on the bench, backed away, paused, then turned to go. Her
costume, always the same, was a skirt of dark material
wrapped several times around her waist and held up by a
narrow belt of red cloth, and a sleeveless blouse covering
the right shoulder. Even though she held her head down,
he could see that her nose stood high and her mouth was
thin and well shaped.

She was called Quail, though a full translation of her
name, Ocelot explained, meant Young-Quail-Who-Dis-
appears-in-Prairie-Grass-and-Whose-Crest-Stands-Above-
the-Grass. This obviously had to be shortened.

She came originally from the hill country of the west,
and her dialect differed from that spoken by the people of
Culhuacan. Salt would ask her the names of things when
she came in the morning, but even as she struggled to
understand him, she refused to raise her eyes.

Having failed to get her to look up, he finally resorted
to a trick. He spent an entire afternoon catching butterflies
of many sizes and colors, and placed them in a little cage
of green willow shoots. When she came the next morning,
he waited until she had set down the tray. Then he pushed
the little cage toward her and popped open its lid. But in
the cool morning air the butterflies were sluggish and
refused to fly up.

The girl looked into the little cage, with its collection

of dormant butterflies. Then she looked squarely at him and began to laugh. They both laughed, and there was never any strangeness between them after that.

Quail had no parents. Her father had been taken as a prisoner of war and, his heart torn from his body, sacrificed on one of the high altars. Her mother died soon afterward, of grief or witchcraft. Two younger brothers were taken by grandparents to rear, but as it was a poor mountain village lying in the path of war parties, the corn and beans raised by the people were frequently seized by one army or another and the people left to await another harvest. Since a girl was a burden to a poor family, Quail was sold and eventually found herself in Tula's household. Here she was well treated and here she hoped to stay for the rest of her life. She told these things in snatches of words, which Salt put together as best he could. Sometimes he had to call upon Ocelot to explain what she told him, but he enjoyed her halting speech and preferred to struggle with it alone. She seemed more willing to talk without a third person present.

The most noticeable thing about her—the tattooed slave mark in the center of her forehead—drew his gaze constantly, but he never asked her about it. It was a small circle, with parallel lines shooting away in the four directions. Though he could not ask about that, he did ask indirect questions about her life.

Salt said to her one day, "Here you will never have your own life. You will have no family, no people of your own."

The girl surprised him with her reply. "Here it is better not to have people of your own. Who can say what bitterness may come to any of us?"

Then she asked in her turn, gaining ease as they talked, "You—and what do you expect to find among these people?"

"Corn! I came to find corn." He had not expected to describe his quest with that single word, but now that he had uttered it, he felt relief. Maybe it was the thing for which he had traveled across mountain and desert. At least it was something the girl would understand.

But she laughed, thinking he had given her a foolish answer.

"Corn," she said after a moment, "you can find anywhere. It must grow everywhere in the world. It even grows in the mountains where I was born."

"It grows in my country also, but hear what troubles we have—" He told her about the dried-up fields, the failing spring, and the corn that seemed to be dying of its own weakness.

And he added, "I have come to find the Mother Corn from which ours came."

Her face brightened. "When I was a child in our mountain village, we sang a song. Maybe it is for you. Listen.

> O sweet light,
> In my eyes see truth.
> O sweet sound,
> In my ears hear truth.
> O sweet mother corn,
> In my heart live truth.

"Maybe this is the Mother Corn you seek."

Salt was pleased.

He had been a guest in Tula's house for many weeks before he ever spoke more than the greetings of the day to the master. Tula was a tall man, of great physical power in spite of advanced years, and a man who obviously exerted authority over the lives of the people around him. His wife had been dead many years and, being an old-fashioned man, as he called himself, he had never remarried. Of his five sons, two had been killed in battle, two were gone to manage farms in distant captured territory, and one lived in the House of the Soldiers in Culhuacan. Three married daughters lived in houses adjoining Tula's city house, but they were usually under Tula's roof with their children, since their husbands were warriors fighting in foreign fields. An ancient woman, Tula's grandmother, or perhaps only an old woman of the clan (Salt could not be sure that he understood the terms of relationship), occupied an apartment to herself and only occasionally came to sun herself in the courtyard.

In addition, a constant stream of guests poured into Tula's house, stayed for a meal or a night's lodging, or remained for weeks. One could never be sure how many people would sit down to the evening table. Tula fed them all. He ate sparingly, but for his guests the serving-women loaded the table with many kinds of meat, baked or cooked in stews; fish served with sweet potatoes; corn flavored with certain herbs and steamed in a husk of leaves; jars of honey and sweet syrup extracted from the maguey plant.

In such a constant crowd, it was not surprising that Salt's

presence should hardly be noticed. But he had come for
a purpose, and he was not content to watch white clouds
sail over the temple on the Hill of the Star or to lose himself in the crowded streets and the public market.

When Tula finally set aside a time for an audience and
notified Salt, he apologized for his neglect. "As you see,
I lead a busy life. It has not been of my own choosing,
but the people of my clan keep me as their spokesman.
We have twenty clans in our tribe, and I represent my clan
in the council of the whole tribe. In addition, I sit as one
of the judges to hear appeals, and sometimes I must argue
these appeals before our High Chief. All of this takes time
and causes me to neglect a man's first duty, which is always
to his guest."

Listening to Tula talk of his duties and responsibilities,
Salt could not understand what Ocelot's father meant when
he spoke of him as a man deprived of power. He wore the
headdress of bright feathers and the purple cape belonging
to a man of high rank. His manner betrayed no uneasiness.
He listened closely, never breaking in while another talked,
never hurrying to finish a conversation.

He showed interest in the things Salt told him. In time,
Tula sensed the perplexity that lay in the mind of the boy
from the north. He invited him to sit at his side at clan
meetings. He took him to visit in the countryside. He
introduced him to priests and military leaders. Salt was
able to visit the schools where boys were trained to be
leaders and warriors.

It must be, Salt thought, that Ocelot's father had forgotten what Tula was like. For here, surely, was a man of

strength, a man of wisdom, a man to whom one would look for help.

No Land of Fable any longer, but a land of men; a land of cities, of buildings, of bridges across lakes, of armies on the march, of temples which thousands of men labored a lifetime in building; a land of cornfields stretching to the skyline; where courts measured out justice; where men were carried in gold-bossed chairs. Not a land of fable, Tula's country.

As Salt looked about, seeking understanding, he remembered the words of the slave girl: "Who knows what bitterness may come to any of us?" What did she mean? Why should anyone speak of bitterness in a land stamped with its own greatness?

Of Tula he asked: "What has made your people powerful? I have only my two hands. What can I carry in them that will help my people to grow strong, as yours have?"

No prompt reply came. The question troubled Tula. He sat in a great square chair, the arms carved into the likeness of gaping snakes, which climbed over the back and entwined their glistening bodies at the top. When Tula was not speaking, he leaned back, and the fingers of his right hand played over the smooth texture of the fangs and nostrils of the snake head.

Salt offered further explanation. "You find it hard to see in your mind what a poor country we have, how weak my people are. The rains no longer come, the crops grow less each year. We have so little, you might expect us to live in peace among ourselves, to share what we have and to support each other. Instead, as I have told you before,

we cut each other down. Our Village Chief can no longer
hold us together, good man that he is. How may we have
peace again? Or must we utterly destroy ourselves?"

Still Tula did not answer. Instead, he rose from his
chair, uttered, "Come!" and strode from the room.

Salt, puzzled, followed. Tula's long strides took him
through the courtyard into the garden with its living fence
of cactus. The land sloped upward to a row of cypress trees
growing across the upper end. Maguey plants in rows
followed the curve of sloping land and Tula walked on
until he came to the topmost part of the garden. There he
waited for Salt.

From that point, the view was across the lake toward the
northeast and the east. Tula moved his arm in an arc con-
necting these two points.

"You can't see what I point out, so you must take my
word for what I tell you. Before you leave this country,
you may even go to see these things for yourself. In any
case, there—" His long, strong finger seemed to poke a
hole in the sky toward the east. "There, in a great dead
city, my people lived, honored their fathers, and kept peace
among themselves. How long ago this was, I cannot tell
you. Our oldest temple priests have no memory of it. Our
tradition tells us that in the city, when our people were
young, our god Quetzalcoatl came to us."

Salt stared into a milk-blue sky without blinking, as if
by the very strength of looking he might bring into view
the dead city of which his host talked. When he took his
eyes away at last, he realized that Tula was staring as if
he could indeed see beyond the horizon.

"I cannot tell you everything that came to us through Quetzalcoatl. I only say this, that the breath which is life, which is seen as a feather on the face of still water, and again in the movement of the Evening Star through the night sky—that is Quetzalcoatl. The least thing, and at once the greatest also. Through his help, our people learned to write upon paper and upon stone. They were told about corn, our Mother—but as I told you, the things we received from him are many and I'll not recount them all."

When he turned away from gazing at the sky, it was as if a shadow fell over his face.

"One thing more, a truth which travels at the side of everything else, as night travels with day, and as death travels at the side of life: man lives in the face of many enemies. His life is a gift, given without his asking, and payment must be made to the giver. A man may try to avoid the payment, but he is a fool if he thinks he can escape and keep the whole gift to himself."

Tula looked up from his speaking as if to satisfy himself that he was understood. His face relented.

"I'm sure that I have talked too hard. You don't have our language fully, so we will return and let your companion help you. Only, before we go—" Tula turned once more to the horizon and pointed southward.

"Off there lies Cholula, the greatest temple in all this land. I hope you will see it."

Tula did not finish everything he wanted to say that first day, but came back to the subject again and again. With Ocelot to help, Salt began to understand that his host was an unhappy man, that he spoke often out of deep bitterness, out of a sense of irredeemable loss. Salt began to understand too what Ocelot's father had meant when he had said that Tula was a man whose power was passing.

In one of these long conversations, Tula said: "Quetzalcoatl, who ruled the lives of our fathers, here in this valley, is not fashionable now. His name is not spoken. Soon even his temples and monuments will be lost. We now have coming from all corners of the world, it seems, a race of men who have neither reason nor shame. Being without reason, they understand nothing; nothing can be explained to them. Being without shame, they are not humble, and cannot be humbled. They think only in terms of size and numbers. The great temples built by our fathers these men covered over, not with masonry and carved stone such as our fathers used, but with the coarsest rocks, even dirt from the fields, so they might have the satisfaction of having built a greater temple!

"That is a vanity they may have—I care nothing about it. But in another matter the change is more serious. These later comers, these men without reason and without shame, are devouring our people. You tell me that your small village is faced with destruction. What if I should tell you that my country, great as it is in people and in land, is destroying itself! Yet, it is so."

In the anxiety of his speech, Tula left his chair often to pace the length of his council hall, along a colonnade of wooden figures bearing the faces of many gods. Blue cloth painted with designs hung against the white walls, and on a central table large bowls, some of dark-brown pottery and some with images of birds and animals worked in gold, were reflected in dark polished wood.

"In former days it was our custom to draw blood from our bodies as a token in payment for the gift of life. This was done with a thorn at many ceremonies. Life must be paid for, and this was a token of our payment. Now come these men, without reason and without shame, these believers in numbers and in size, and they turn the simple ceremonies of our fathers into spectacles of horror. Our temples are washed in blood. Each year great throngs of our own people, as well as armies of captive tribes, are slaughtered.

"And here am I, Tula. My name is the name of my race. I am the head of my clan and spokesman for my clan in the Supreme Council of all the people. Yet I am helpless to hold back this tide which sweeps over us. I have many brother tribesmen who believe as I do in the older religion, but all of us together are powerless to save our people from destruction.

"So when you ask me how to save your village, I can only turn and ask, how may I save my own people?"

Tula's words, as Salt absorbed their cumulative effect, were sufficiently shattering. But they would have ended as words; nothing would have come of them, if it had not been for what Tula finally said, almost casually, as if it had slipped his mind:

"We are soon to celebrate the Feast of the Eighth Month. Perhaps you do not know this feast . . . in which the maturing of the new corn is honored by cutting off the head of a young girl . . . in the sight of the multitude . . .

"Well, we shall have the feast. And my household has been commanded to deliver an honored victim. I am powerless. Up to now, I have evaded these demands. If I continue to evade, I may lose my entire family, my sons and daughters, and my own life, useless as it is."

Salt was frightened. All that Tula had been saying became clear at last. This pleasant house, the pleasant sunshine in the courtyard, turned deathly cold. He shivered and would have turned away, to hear no more. But too late. Tula had been gazing at him; now he looked away. His words fell like petals from a dead flower.

"I have consented. The girl who came to us from the mountains—whom we call Quail—she will go to the temple and be sacrificed."

A parrot screamed in the courtyard. Even the distant barking of a dog pierced Salt's consciousness. But these sensations were detached from him. His mind and spirit had fled his mute body. So he stood, wounded deeply, wordless.

When thought unfroze at last and he could look upon Tula and upon the things standing in the room, he knew that his quest in behalf of his people had ended, here. He had not found the power that would help them; he would not find it; not here, not in death.

Tula, having finally unburdened himself, walked from the room, his stiff back suggesting the aloofness of the defeated.

Salt watched Tula go and hoped that he would never again have to speak with him.

Chapter 17

Flight from the Valley of Bitterness

OCELOT was terrified when Salt came to him with his plan. In the depth of the night, Salt had awakened Ocelot by placing his hand over his friend's mouth. In whispers the mad plan was broached: "The mountain girl is to be killed unless we save her."

That was how it started. Ocelot protested; he would have no part of it. He explained the dangers, the almost certain death. He explained the distances that must be traveled before they would be beyond the reach of Culhuacan soldiers. Even Tula would be bound to use his clansmen against them. As a slave, with the slave's mark tattooed on her forehead, no household would dare take them in, no one could protect them.

They talked most of that night, in whispers no louder than the sound of the wind in the leaves of the pepper trees. Salt would not be moved from his decision. Ocelot's pleading turned to anger, and finally into a threat of exposing the plan.

To everything, Salt made the steadfast reply: "Tula himself would do this if he could. He is unhappy about the girl. We do this for Tula."

Salt did not believe this, but he tried to will it to be true.

To which Ocelot replied over and over, "Then let Tula do it."

In the morning they went up through the town, saying nothing, but marking the streets and roads they would follow, the traps they must avoid.

In midafternoon, as they sat on a grass slope high above the city, the lake spread out before them, Ocelot remarked, without previous indication that he had even been thinking about the matter: "We must have a canoe ready. We could never make it by land. We would be caught at the bridge, if not before. We will have to go by water."

No more was said. They went down the hill, knowing that they would work together. At Tula's house they separated, Ocelot saying that he would go to find a canoe, while Salt went to the market to trade cacao beans for food and the articles they would need for the journey.

Tula was not present at the evening meal, and the boys

were saved the embarrassment of conversing with him. Salt dreaded a meeting. His anger at Tula, added to the fear he felt, made him unsure of himself.

They must start that night. Salt knew this. If they calculated their chances, tried to plan more carefully, they might lose their courage. When he realized that Ocelot was of the same mind, his spirits rose. They waited together for the summer twilight to pass and the night to arrive. Neither spoke, but each feared the moment when they must act. So at last they came to the point of action.

The greatest danger lay at the very outset. No man, other than an immediate member of the family, might enter the women's quarters. To be found there was to risk instant death.

Every large house had its own watchman, to guard against prowlers, watch for fires, easily started in a community of thatched roofs. He also watched for falling stars and other portents in the night sky that might bear upon the fortunes of the household.

The watchman in Tula's house was an ancient soldier with one eye, but a sharp eye. He often remained motionless for hours on end, leaning against a wall or tree. He seemed to have no regular sleeping time, but when he tired he might lie down on a rush mat near the street entrance. At all cost, they must avoid an encounter with him.

The last-quarter moon would not rise until after the middle of the night, a point in their favor when they started. Waiting just outside his door, Salt heard his heart pound. His hand touched Ocelot close by. Then they moved forward. The guard, they hoped, was stretched out asleep on his mat.

Salt knew where the girl slept, sharing her room with a single companion, an older woman. They crept out of the courtyard into the women's quarters.

Ocelot waited at Quail's door when Salt slipped inside. In the windowless room, utter darkness faced him. He was not sure where the sleeping pallets were. Most likely, toward the back. He dropped to his knees, crept forward.

Sweeping his hands before him, he touched a pallet. But whose? He leaned as far forward as he dared, sniffing at the air. A sour, forbidding odor.

Across the room, then. Again he sniffed. Now he smiled. The girl's breath was like the sage at dawn. He put his hand to her mouth; even that did not waken her at once. But when he squeezed her nostrils together, she gave a start.

Lying in the darkness, explaining why he had come and what he wanted her to do, it seemed to Salt he could never make her understand or persuade her to move. She offered no response at all, not even to indicate that she heard.

At the door, meantime, Ocelot rubbed his thumb over his fingertips, making a dry whisper. Was he urging speed, or warning of danger?

Just as Salt decided to crawl to the doorway and learn the reason for the signal, Quail shook her head affirmatively and began to rise. Her hand fumbled in the darkness, drawing a pouch from under her pallet. But Salt, in his eagerness to be away, did not observe this movement. He went quickly and found Ocelot crouching just inside the doorway.

He caught the whispered warning: "Stay low. I think One-Eye comes this way."

Hardly had he given the warning when they heard the footstep just beyond the open door. Had Ocelot's whisper carried out there? Salt, crouching opposite, dared not move, even to warn Quail. He feared she would come forward and, by whispered word or otherwise, reveal their presence. The watchman must be standing just outside. Time dragged so slowly.

When Quail did come, she was as stealthy as night itself. She touched him; otherwise he might not have felt her presence.

The girl seemed to sense the reason for their waiting. After a moment, she pressed her hand on Salt's shoulder, signaling him to stay. She rose to her feet and stepped through the doorway.

Too late, Salt realized what she was doing. If he had sensed it sooner, he would have pulled her back. She was gone, leaving him terrified.

But she had reasoned soundly. The watchman could not have suspected her action. It was her room, and she was free to get up during the night.

When she found no one outside, the boys could not be sure whether they had imagined a presence or whether the guard had moved to another vantage point and might still be waiting.

Now it was time to move. Ocelot, bending low, went
first; then Quail; then Salt. They reached the entrance to
the garden. Nothing happened.

Then, running feet! A shout!

No word was needed. As one, the three raced down the
long rows of maguey plants. The direction of their flight
had not yet been noticed. The torches blooming into sudden
light were still within the courtyard. They had reached
the far end of the garden and were slashing a hole through
the cactus fence when the first torch entered the garden
behind them.

Their wild flight led them away from the lake and the
spot where Ocelot had hidden the canoe. They had to
backtrack, keeping to a wide circle, and risk an encounter
with townsmen or soldiers attracted by the lights and the
shouts at Tula's house. They ran on, staying in the shadow
of the walls and trees. Several times they lost themselves
in roads and alleyways that ended dead against a house or
high wall.

But it was a relief to be running, to be away. The long
journey ahead concerned Salt not at all.

Waiting in shadow while Ocelot scouted ahead, Salt explained what he had been told by Tula. So far he had been
able to tell Quail only that her life was threatened, and
she must escape. When she understood that she had been
destined to perform in the Eighth Month ceremony, cele-
brating the ripening of the corn, she whispered:

"But that is a great honor! In that ceremony a slave
girl rises above all the people in the nation. She gives her
life to bring a good harvest."

Astonishing words! They left Salt feeling foolish. Was it possible that she preferred to stay and enjoy the honor? He realized how little he understood this girl, or the people in this strange land. How foolish to expect strangers to be like his own people!

As he puzzled, he heard soft laughter. He turned to the girl; she had put her hand over her mouth to suppress her mirth.

"It *is* an honor. But I am happy to pass it on to somebody else. Did you think I wished to go back?"

Salt floundered. "You spoke of bitterness one day. I thought that meant that you would escape if you could. But just now—I was lost. It is better to live, I think."

"Yes, it is better to live. But I just now thought of that. If you had not asked me to come, the other would have seemed all right, I guess. One changes."

While they talked, Ocelot had been motioning them from a shadowing hedge. He had to come halfway across the open space and hiss sharply before they were aware of him.

Then they were running again, down a long incline leading to the water's edge. Ocelot, still beckoning, crept along a marshy shore to the hiding place of the canoe. Breathless, they came up with him and found him staring at a place where the reeds had been flattened. Only muddy water showed.

The canoe was gone! Frightened, they looked at each other. In growing panic, each ran in a different direction, plunging in among the tall reeds and sinking in the muddy ooze.

A moment later, Ocelot called. They found him laughing. He had been looking for the canoe in the wrong place. Now he had found it just where he left it.

By the time they pushed away from the shore, the summer dawn was almost upon them. A mist would be upon the lake at daylight, and they could hope to go unobserved. When they were well out from shore, Salt untied the bundle at his waist and brought out a skirt and blouse. These he had bought at the market, paying in cacao beans taken from Tula's house. The girl threw her old garments into the water. He could think of no way for her to cover the tattoo mark on her forehead, but when daylight came he discovered that she had plaited her hair in two braids and wrapped them around her head so that nothing showed.

Paddling southward, they kept well away from either shore. The mist was not as heavy as usual, but there was enough to curtain them from the land. However, it would lift when the sun warmed the air, and they must leave the water before that happened. They drove the canoe into a narrow inlet, where a stream poured down from a mountain headland.

Now they were with danger again. They must travel for many days through a countryside, well peopled, and risk encounter with soldiers or agents of Culhuacan or of Tula himself. A slave, at any time, was not given up easily. A slave who had been chosen by the temple for its uses would be searched for with diligence. Tula would certainly be accused of plotting Quail's escape; he would make a special effort to find her and bring her back.

With the canoe well hidden, the three fugitives crawled into the underbrush along the stream bed. There they stayed all through the heat of that first day. They watched the herons stand motionless, then stab the muck for a frog morsel. Ducks streaked low over the water, seeking a feeding ground. Gulls rose from a distant headland, complaining, headed toward the outer lake, then tilted upward, swerved, still complaining, returned shoreward, and finally came to rest riding high in the water.

Salt turned to the girl: "Where will you go? Will you be safe among your people in the mountains?"

Quail had given it thought, and her answer came at once. "I have no people."

Ocelot passed out food, a tortilla and a portion of beancake to each. "My family will be happy to have you. You will be one of us, not a slave."

Salt looked at the girl but could not tell how she would respond. She would do well to accept; she would be safe. A place would be made for her. But he hoped she would not accept, or would put off a decision. He could not say why he wanted this, since he had nothing to suggest in its place.

To Ocelot he remarked: "Your father is Tula's friend. He may not want to offend Tula by taking this girl."

A hard quality came into Ocelot's voice. "Perhaps you want to take her with you, through the desert and mountains?"

The question startled Salt. He had given it no thought, but he answered, "Perhaps. It will be up to her."

Ocelot's voice had softened again when he said, "My father will not let her return, even to Tula, when he understands what they would do to her."

The girl had not looked up while they talked. Now she spread her hands as if to end the talk. "We have not escaped yet. Who knows whether we will? We can talk about this again."

That evening they left their shelter and climbed a sloping hill. Presently they came upon a trail leading inland and followed it. The trail joined a road northward. Following along it, they soon came to the edge of the town of Cuecuilco.

There, for a moment, their adventure seemed to come to an end.

Since darkness was rapidly approaching, they walked with less caution. They knew a town was close at hand, but had not realized how close. They emerged from a grove of trees and found that the road had become a street lined with houses. Should they continue through the town, or seek a way around? Pausing to consider, they saw figures emerge from the shadows of the buildings. They were surrounded before they could turn.

A voice accosted them, "Run now and you run into trouble." The voice, gruff and familiar, startled Salt. Impossible to believe!

The speaker advanced until he was close upon them. Beyond doubt, it was the one-eyed watchman.

The voice was a growl. "I saw you run to the canoe and guessed where you would come ashore. A little waiting—and here you are."

Salt urged: "Let the girl go! Say you have not seen her!"

The watchman waved his words aside. "I know nothing of this. I only come with a message from Tula. I am to give you the names of the towns you will pass through, and the names of clansmen who will provide food and keep you out of sight during the day. You must travel only at night."

The three stood motionless and speechless, trying to understand. Was it a trap? Was One-Eye leading them into an ambush?

"Well?" the one-eyed soldier exploded. "Are you listening?"

The spell broke. Yes, indeed, they listened!

To Salt, the listing of towns and individuals was wasted effort. He could not distinguish one from the other. All names in this strange land were a confusion to him. But he heard Ocelot and Quail murmuring the words, fastening them in their memories.

Salt still groped for understanding. "This is strange. The girl was demanded by the temple. Tula's family will be destroyed if he withholds the girl. . ."

"You are foolish, man from the north. Why did he tell you about the girl? He could not keep her back himself, but if you steal her, how can he help it? Only, I warn you, if you are caught, you will go to the sacrificial stone with the girl. That is my message, and now you have not seen me."

Salt had to ask, "Did you see us leave, then?"

Even suggesting that he might not have seen them was

an insult to One-Eye's vigilance. "Nothing happens at
Tula's house that I do not see!" The watchman turned at
that and went back into the shadows, and the shadowy
forms with him were no more.

Now that they could travel with some security, Salt
should have carried a light heart, but as they plodded
through the nights that followed, sadness overwhelmed
him. He had failed his people. He had been chosen from
all the men of his village to find the secret that would
save his people. He had found no secret, and in his concern
to rescue the slave girl, he had not even gathered the corn
that grew in this land. He was empty-handed.

During the daylight hours, while they rested at the
home of one of Tula's clansmen, Salt would lie and stare
at thatched roof or sky, whichever happened to be overhead, when he should have slept. Not only was he troubled
by his failure to find a word or a sign that would protect
his people, but more seriously was he troubled by a growing sense that such a secret sign or word did not exist in
the world. He remembered, when he asked what he could
do to save his village, how Tula had turned the question
back on him. Surely if there was a way for men to live
without destroying each other, the people of Culhuacan
should have found it. With their rich clothes and ornaments, their abundance of food, their marching armies,
their courts and their judges, their towering pyramids and
smoking temples—surely they should have found how
men may live together in peace and support each other.

Was it possible, as Tula suggested, that in a more ancient

time men had lived in peace, had paid for the gift of life with orderliness and decency, and had been overwhelmed by ruder men and ruder ideas?

He asked Ocelot: "Do your people live in fear of your temples? Are your priests smeared with people's blood?"

And Ocelot replied: "We fear only the people in the land where we have just been. They would destroy us, if they could, demand our crops and our men. My father tells me this, and that is why he feared for our going. We keep a guard on our border, as you shall see."

Salt felt that his question had not been answered, but he did not pursue it further. Perhaps the other had never reflected on the questions that bothered him.

Not many days later, they reached an outpost such as Ocelot had mentioned—a square stone building on the edge of a low bluff that overlooked a narrow mountain pass. Below it were stone barracks for the guards. Salt remembered it from the previous spring, but now the outpost took on a new meaning.

For now, at last, they could travel openly in the daylight, without fear. They were beyond the reach of the soldiers of Culhuacan!

A great valley opened out, bounded by rising mountains, timbered and green, while in the middle distance sharp cones rose up, timbered over also, which once had spilled molten rock and burning ash over the countryside. A scene of peace, with cornfields far below, a stream that curved upon itself, and a family of crows moving on the wing.

It was the moment that Salt had been waiting for, the moment when they should have passed beyond danger. He turned to Quail and saw that her eyes were filled with the peace that lay before them. Even her nostrils seemed to quiver, taking it in. Up to then, she had walked wearily, in tattered garments, never falling behind, but never exulting.

Now they were here, beyond the threat of death, and he asked her: "We said we would not speak of this again until we came to safety. This is Ocelot's green country. Soon we will come to his lake. What have you thought? Will you stay here, where they will make a place for you? Or will you continue with me to my people, where the land is poor, where the rains seem to come no more, and where we live without peace?"

The girl still looked lingeringly at the far-off green mountains, then turned her gaze on Salt. He stood a head taller. His expression, she had come to know, was always serious. He was thinner than he should be, but his strength was tireless. He seemed ready to go on forever, searching for whatever it was that his spirit needed.

She watched him a moment, then said: "I have thought about this ever since we left the lake shore. Indeed, I thought about it as I left my bed in Tula's house. You asked me to come with you, and I will go wherever you go."

Ocelot was not displeased. "This boy from the north will never be frightened. I never expected to survive that night, but he would not turn back. It is best that you go with him. We will rest in my father's house first. With permission, I will go with you as far as the salt water, where our boundaries lie."

Chapter 18

Village of the White Rocks

SALT would have hurried on, without resting, if that had been possible. From the time they came in sight of the salt water and said their farewells to Ocelot, Salt thought only of home. He would push out of mind the images of flood-swollen rivers, of thorny brush, of waterless deserts and days of hunger. He would think of nothing but the village in the canyon. Who had died? Who was in power? How did the crops grow?

Before they had traveled far up the coast, they met the

221

first of many delays. It was the season of summer rains, and the rivers were in flood again. He remembered the long plain that ran along the coast, where the people built their houses on mounds of earth. Now he understood why. The road had disappeared under water, and every village, every house, was an island to itself. He scouted up and down the swampy shore, trying to find a roadway.

Here the mountains rose abruptly only a short distance back from the salt water; their sides were covered with an impassable tangle of thorny growth. After days, while Salt's despair mounted, a single canoeman came within shouting distance, and the boy negotiated by many signs and useless words. The Indian in the dugout canoe, dubious at first, agreed to ferry them across the water and set them on their way. But at parting, he talked volubly, pointing northward.

Two days later they understood what the canoeman meant. The road disappeared under a second flooded area.

The first several weeks passed in that manner. Even when he and Quail traveled on high ground, the drenching rains fell each afternoon and left them floundering in mud. When the rains swept on down the coast, the sun burned away the sodden clouds and they gasped for breath in the hot steam.

Delays and discomforts only made Salt drive the harder. He built canoes or rafts, stole them when that was possible, and negotiated when he had to.

When they came to Culiacan, Salt walked warily through the streets, hoping he would not meet the judge-priest or Yucca Flower Woman. Hospitality would require a feast, and a delay that could grow into many days. Yet he needed to visit the market, since Quail's and his sandals and clothing were falling apart. Also, he remembered the fluted brown pottery in the market and thought of his mother. She would be happy with such a gift. He traded cacao beans, since these were as much relished at Culiacan as they were in the country of the lakes.

Now they traveled inland away from the sea. The country grew drier and more forbidding. The road narrowed to a track; a desolation of impenetrable brush crept upon the trail from either side.

In the long march that followed, across swollen rivers and intervening stretches of waterless rough country, Salt learned a deeper appreciation of the girl who followed. In his driving desire to cover ground, to surmount obstacles, forever to be moving forward, he would often forget her. He never once slowed for her convenience, and rarely did he think to ask if she needed rest. However hard he drove, she was never far behind.

When they stopped to prepare a meal, he might say: "We still have far to go. We must hurry."

She would answer: "I know you are hungry for home. Go as hard as you can. I will follow."

He had left the Village of the White Rocks in the first days of summer. A second summer had passed, and now the time of the winter rains was approaching when Salt and the girl found the headwaters of the north-flowing river that would take them to the land of the big fields.

They spent two days at that place, because Salt wanted to see again how the ditches were dug to lead water from the river. He ran the soil through his fingers and fed his eyes on the spaciousness of the flat valley. The corn was gone from the fields and meadow grass lay brown, but even so the land did not look dead. Cool air descending from the mountains lay in a pleasant haze over the countryside.

To Quail he said: "Here could dwell a great people, with abundant harvests, such as we left down there in the Valley of the Lakes. But here a people could live in peace, as well, and not be burdened with temples crying for blood."

Quail's face had thinned, the cheekbones showing sharply, and her eyes in this thinness looked larger. Turning to her, Salt saw in her eyes the same look of peace that glowed in them when, from a mountaintop, they looked down into the green valley bordering Ocelot's country. He had been troubled back there, believing that she had found in that pleasant country the world of her desire, and that he would lose her.

Now she saw what he saw—the standing fields, the flashing water, the crowned cottonwood trees struck golden. She turned to him, the same pleasant longing shining from her eyes.

She echoed the very thought that lay in his mind. "Here," she said, "*your* people could grow strong. And you would have peace."

A true thing, if he had not come empty-handed from the Red Land of the South.

He explained: "Our Holy One could not tell me what to bring. I was to use my eyes. But failing all else, I should have brought new corn to replace our tired seed. I waited too long, always thinking I would find something hidden. So I left with nothing in my hands."

Quail smiled, for the first time, he thought, since they talked in Tula's house; a weak smile, burdened by fatigue and the dust of traveling.

"You are not empty-handed," she said. "See, I brought this—"

As she spoke, she unfastened a small leather pouch from her belt, the pouch she had drawn from under the pallet as she rose to follow Salt. In all this journey it had remained unopened.

"You spoke once of this very thing—and I gathered these few kernels from each of the strong corns that grow in the Valley of the Lakes. Who would believe that I myself would carry them to your country!"

On her outspread skirt, she spilled the pouch of corn— and Salt was astonished. Until then he had known only yellow corn. But here were kernels of red, blue, and black corn, and a yellow kernel larger than any he had ever seen. They sparkled, as if alive, in the haze-blurred sun.

Truly he had learned at last to appreciate this girl who had followed so faithfully.

They rose then, crossed the river, and went up into the mountains.

On a day when frost weighed heavily upon dead meadow grass and strands of snow clouds flew like ribbons around

mountain peaks, Salt and Quail came to the valley of his
people. And when, in the gray light of a dying day, they
saw the new village in the bottom of the canyon, it seemed
indeed a cramped and narrow place.

Salt turned to Quail: "Perhaps you will regret that you
came. You see how small it is."

And she answered: "You saw how I lived in a world
that was big. Who knows but what a lesser place will have
more room for me."

Word had gone on ahead, and the Holy One came out
to meet them. Yes, the Holy One still lived! Salt saw the
old man at the head of all the villagers, his white hair
gleaming in the deepening dusk. He came, hurrying a
little, his legs showing unsteadiness. His hands hung low,
palms outward, and as he came near he half raised them
in a sign of wonder.

Salt and Quail then stood side by side.

The Holy One looked first at the boy, then at the girl.
He spoke the first words.

"You may bring gifts of power from the south; you may
bring gifts of peace for our people. We will ask of that
in due time. Whatever else, truly you have brought a gift
of beauty in this girl. We will be happy in her."

And it seemed to be even so.

Salt's mother looked at the girl, and was happy. The
people took her up to the village, into the warmth of the
fires, and whoever looked at her felt a pleasure and a
happiness. They murmured, in quietness away from her
hearing, "The mark of the sun is upon her, there on her
forehead. Have you seen it?"

Salt thought to speak of this. He turned to the Holy One, forming the words in his mind. Then he looked at the girl who was called Young-Quail-Who-Disappears-in-Prairie-Grass-and-Whose-Crest-Stands-Above-the-Grass. She stood with the firelight upon her. Her eyes had never been so full of longing as they were then. Never had the vision of peace so filled them.

The words he would have uttered, explaining the slave mark, dissolved and were gone. The mark itself—the little circle, with parallel lines running to the four directions—glowed brightly as the girl stood before the firelight. And the people spoke in wonder.

Weariness fell away from Salt's limbs, and from his heart as well. The disappointment which had been building so steadily since he left Tula's house, tasting so bitter, was fading like a dream at waking time.

People began to come forward, out of the shadows beyond the fire. Shield, thin as always, his eyes deep in their sockets, placed his hand on Salt's shoulder.

"Our grandson is indeed a man among us. We rejoice in you."

Then Trailing Cloud, the ancient Sun Watcher, came leaning on a younger arm. He too reached out to touch Salt.

"My eyes have lasted until now—and for that I am thankful—that I may see once more our clansman. We will grow great again in your lifetime. Our people will survive in you."

Then out of the crowd came one, the sight of whom made Salt's heart leap up. Day Singer was before him—

an eye destroyed, an angry red scar slashing down his face
from hairline to chin. His graying hair, as always, was
bound in a twist of red cotton cloth. Their hands met.

"The circle is complete, grandson." It was an old-
fashioned way of expressing happiness.

Salt murmured: "I can see how the circle almost ended
for you, in the kiva of the Spider Clan."

"Almost. For Turtle, that was the end."

The note of sorrow burned for a moment, and still
smoldered as others came forward, expressing happiness.

While the joy of reunion mounted to fullness, a strange
thing happened. Who first called out, was not known.
Simply a voice beyond the firelight.

"Take guard! A stranger approaches!"

Talking broke off. All turned to look.

What they saw, at the farthest reach of the firelight,
was startling.

A man stood there, just visible in the darkness. A man
they first took to be in death-mourning. His long hair,
loosened from its binding cloth, fell wildly over face and
shoulders. All ornaments had been stripped from his body;
he walked barefooted, his only garment a breechclout.

He approached within view, then waited to be asked to
come forward.

The Holy One must have suspected at once. He stood
away from the others and cried out:

"Whoever you are, here you are welcome."

The shadowy one advanced, and a gasp went up like a
burst of wind through a pine grove.

Dark Dealer stood there among them, head bowed, waiting to be invited to speak.

"Do you come in friendship?" the Holy One asked, hardness in his voice.

The reply was long in emerging, then: "A second winter is upon us. Our food will soon be gone. Let our women and children come to you. Our men you may wish to punish for striking you. Me, you may feed to the vultures. I am ready."

Voices rose, murmuring, then in loud anger.

"This is a trick!"

"Who can believe him?"

"Send him back to his den of coyotes!"

The Holy One held up his hands, asking silence. But he did not give the answer to Dark Dealer. Instead, he turned to Salt.

"This night, and our future, belong to our grandson. Let him say what we are to do."

The words lighted a glow in the boy's eyes, like sunlight bursting upon a dark morning. Often on a lonely night he had dreamed of the time when he would be asked, as a man, to speak for his people. Now the time had come, on the heels of failure too! Joy could be no sweeter! But, as he prepared to speak, he thought again of the man Tula, and it was as if a tempering hand rested on his shoulder.

"It is not for us to say whether any man has lived his life well," he ventured, and as he spoke his voice grew stronger. "Each man can answer only for himself. If Dark Dealer finds in his heart that he has not done well, and asks us to take him back, we cannot refuse. We cannot deny him his chance to make the gift which will fulfil his life. I say, bring them all back, and make our people whole again."

Dark Dealer, wordless, dropped to his knees before Salt. His right hand moved, scooping dirt. With head on knees, he poured dust on his matted hair. It was the supreme submission.

The people watched, awed into silence. Never had they expected to see Dark Dealer at their feet.

Crane Woman, the bold speaker, voiced the wonder and doubt they felt.

"What has brought this about? Not hunger alone. This man was proud beyond the reach of hunger. Yet, here he is, in the dust. I cannot understand it."

Bold speaking was proper in Crane Woman at last, since she was now called Eldest Woman, taking her place in her generation.

"I think understanding is here among us," the Holy One spoke, when no one else offered. He had been standing back; now he came forward to Salt's shoulder. The firelight caught in his eyes, where it burned brightly.

"We sent this boy out at a time when we were troubled. Murder had occurred. We were thrown out of our village. I, your leader, had failed. Now this boy returns, and at almost that moment our enemy comes with bowed head. Did he watch from the mesa top and plan his return to be with us in our moment of our rejoicing, when we might be expected to relent? I find it impossible to believe."

The old man searched the faces before him, turning

slowly. He stood slightly lower than Salt and had to reach up to place his hand on the boy's shoulder.

"It is not strange, I think, for our enemy to seek us out at this time. The power in this boy has pulled him—"

The Holy One was looking directly at Salt, studying his face, his high, thin nose, his quiet eyes.

"Power is here. The power to restore peace in a bad heart. The very power needed by our people."

The Holy One turned again, his hand still on Salt's shoulder, but his eyes seeking the girl Quail.

"If we ask ourselves how this power comes to this boy, I find that answer not strange either. Here is this girl, bearing some sign, perhaps of the sun, on her brow. Bring her here, where we can look upon her."

Quail, standing among the women, her fingers locked together, would have protested. She felt herself still to be the girl who had gone to sleep in the women's quarters at Tula's house, who had been awakened in the dark, and had risen to follow the boy from the north. If greatness existed, it was in him, as he pushed on among enemies, in strange desert lands. All this she would have protested, but the Holy One was calling her forward, giving her no occasion to speak.

Presently she stood beside Salt; and the people, gazing upon her, saw the mark upon her brow, and the wide, longing look in her eyes.

Then they drew closer, as if pulling sheltering walls around her.

The Holy One was saying: "We will call her Red Corn Woman, honoring the south, which sent her to us. With

this name we make her one of us, and her strength will
be ours."

"This is true," the people answered. "She will be one
of us. We feel her strength entering into us."

Salt, looking across space, saw the slave girl vanish, and
beauty stand before him. His smile shone back from her
eyes.

Then he spoke for her, since in all that time she had
not raised her voice: "You honor yourselves in letting this
girl come among you. She will never fall behind. She will
never weary. Her devotion is as a river coming down from
the mountains. All this is her power, and it will help us to
grow great. But if more is needed—why, only look at what
she carries in this little pouch tied to her belt."

Quail would still have protested, but when Salt stretched
out his hand, her agitation was calmed.

"These few seeds—" she said, breaking her silence. She
looked up then, and when she saw how warmly the people
held her in their eyes, her heart was overwhelmed. She
could not speak again.

This was the manner of Salt's return to his village. The
people were reunited, but those who had built houses in
the canyon did not return to their dwellings in the cliff.
The canyon bottom sheltered them against the high winds
of winter, and the women discovered that their lives were
less burdened when they did not have to carry water jars
up a steep trail.

But the people did not remain for long in the Canyon

of the White Rocks. They planted the corn, the "few seeds" which Quail brought with her, murmuring their astonishment at the color and plumpness of the seed. And it flourished, giving them more food than they had known in many seasons.

It came too late, however. The years had been growing drier in Salt's lifetime, and there came a succession of seasons when no rain fell, the spring ceased to flow at summer's peak, and they almost lost even the precious new seed.

Salt, at last, made the decision which changed the lives of his people. He was then Village Chief, succeeding the Holy One, who named him as he lay dying, on a day in winter when the sun stood frozen in a thin cloud.

The memory of green fields, crowned cottonwoods, and running water had remained with Salt. When he called the people together and asked if they would follow him, they lamented the choice, but agreed.

"After all," he reminded them, "our Red Corn Woman saw this land with me. The wonder of it is still in her eyes."

It softened the blow of removal, knowing that she would be with them. For she had grown close to the people, caring for the aged, speaking softly to the young.

So they left the Canyon of the White Rocks, which today stands tenantless and soundless. They traveled southward, down from the mountains, into the valley of the big fields. Land was set aside for them by those who were there first, and the new corn, when planted and watered abundantly, produced such harvests as had never been known. In their rejoicing the people performed a new ceremony, which they called Red Corn Dance. In time they built a great village of adobe walls, and dug canals to lead water from the river to their planted fields.

There they lived in peace and supported one another.

Afterword
by Alfonso Ortiz

O NE of D'Arcy McNickle's favorite stories during the last fifteen years or so of his life concerned an experience he had with a Canadian Cree student at the University of Saskatchewan's Regina campus. D'Arcy was the founding chairman of the Department of Anthropology there, and he had this student in a survey course on Indians of the Americas. When D'Arcy came to the part in his course about the civilizations of Mesoamerica, he showed slides of the temples and pyramids to accompany his lectures.

The young Cree student, who had heretofore sat quietly in the back of the class, suddenly began to show an extraordinary interest in the slides and discussions of Mesoamerica. Yet when that portion of the course was over, he suddenly disappeared. Day

after day, week after week, his seat remained empty
that winter. Then, less than a month after he left the
course, he suddenly reappeared, looking tan and relaxed. D'Arcy was, understandably, not pleased, as
the young man had missed a lot of classes, so he had
him stay after class that day to explain himself. The
student related how he had become fascinated with
the monumental architecture of Mesoamerica, and
with the idea that Indians had erected those struc-
tures, and so he had decided to hitch-hike down there
to see them for himself. On the way back, he had
hitch-hiked up the West Coast of the United States,
all in less than a month!

This story is not apocryphal, and D'Arcy retold it
regularly to new listeners after he left the university.
I think he saw in this young Cree a latter-day and
real "runner in the sun." This story and my other
comments are intended to help readers understand
this delightful novel, and to know something of D'Arcy
McNickle, the man, and of the times during which
he wrote.

When one reads *Runner in the Sun* for the first
time, one cannot help but feel a bit puzzled, as it
seems to stand quite apart from D'Arcy's other writings. McNickle is well known for two other powerful
novels, *The Surrounded* and *Wind from an Enemy
Sky,* novels in which the conflict between white and
Indian cultures is vividly depicted, and the sense of
inevitable tragedy lingers in one's mind long after the
novels are finished. *Runner* is far removed both in

space and time from the other novels. The story is set among the "cliff dwellers," prehistoric Pueblo Indians of the Southwest, long before Columbus happened upon the Americas. At first blush, the novel might be taken as escapist literature, as it was written during the first years of the termination era of the 1950s, an especially tense and difficult time for the Indian tribes of this nation. This view might be reinforced by the fact that the novel was written originally for a juvenile audience.

However, anyone who knew D'Arcy at all well knows that it was not like him to write escapist literature. But this still begs the question: Why *did* he choose to write and publish a novel such as *Runner* in 1954? He had already been working on what would later become *Wind from an Enemy Sky* for about fifteen years, years during which he bemoaned the fact that he did not have the time to finish it. Why, then, did he drop that novel for a time to write *Runner* instead? The answer, I believe, is that *Runner* is not so very different in the concerns it expresses from the concerns the author expressed in his other writings, both fiction and nonfiction.

The story narrated here is simple. Salt, a young Indian boy, is sent on a long journey southward in search of something—we know not what until the end—that may save his people, who are threatened by poverty, drought, and discord from within. Salt returns, in due time, carrying with him a new, higher-yielding breed of corn, but this is only one of the messages in the novel. In his own foreword, D'Arcy strikes a "they came here first" theme, a theme which is not only embodied in the title of his book on the history of the Indians of the Americas, but one which he sounded regularly in his writings after World War II. The theme refers to the modest—and true—proposition that Columbus did not so much discover the Americas as the Americas discovered him, he being the one who was lost. Furthermore, the history of the Americas did not begin with Columbus, as there was a rich human history here—albeit one not written down in an alphabet-based language—before the extension of European history to these shores. Yet it is a story and a history that Euro-Americans have never acknowledged and accepted as predating their own. Hence, D'Arcy begins his own foreword as follows: "Most of us grow up believing that the history of America begins with the men who came across from Europe and settled in the New World wilderness. The real story of our country is much older, much richer than this usual history book account." Later he adds, "They were real people,"—not legend. They existed on this same earth: "They lived, looking into the very skies we look into, hundreds of years before Columbus and his three little ships set sail from Isabella's Spain."

Indeed, the book repeatedly reaffirms the antiquity of the Indian people. Since they *were* here first, they are entitled to stay on their land and to survive as a people, culturally as well as physically. In this regard,

Runner addresses the toughest challenge to face Indian people during the years when it was being written, their right to survive as a people. This, I believe, was D'Arcy's response to the tragic policy of termination. *Runner,* therefore, is not simply an innocent book for juveniles, although juveniles can always read it for profit and pleasure. Rather, D'Arcy is claiming for Indian people a reality apart from that granted to them by white people, and it is a reality whites cannot erase nor, eventually, fail to face.

In 1954 D'Arcy published two major articles in addition to *Runner,* and the three works are closely related. In an article published in the magazine *Americas,* D'Arcy observes:

> It has been a matter of constant astonishment to the Europeans who have been coming to the Western Hemisphere since the close of the fifteenth century that New World inhabitants did not rush upon them with open arms like lost children, and avail themselves of the knowledge, skills, and customs of what the Europeans had always thought of as the older and more advanced culture. The very term "New World" is a European concept implying that life in the Americas had no depth of antiquity and, therefore, had acquired no importance in world history.

In his own foreword D'Arcy describes the first Americans in the following terms: "They were skilled craftsmen and artists. . . . Some were fishermen and sea-mammal hunters. . . . Others were renowned hunters of land animals. But by far the greater part of this population depended upon agriculture, and

some groups even constructed irrigation works to reclaim otherwise worthless desert lands."

To demonstrate the continuity of D'Arcy's vision
and concerns to the very end of his life, I summarize
now the major points of a lecture he gave at his birth-
place on the Flathead Reservation of Montana in the
summer of 1977. It was the last lecture he ever gave,
and it represented a homecoming for D'Arcy in the
most sublime sense, for it was the first time he had
been on the Flathead in fifty years, or since he originally left. In his talk, D'Arcy gave an accounting of
the things he had learned in all of that time away.
He mentioned some of the common ideas about Indians which he encountered, and which are the big-
gest obstacles "in the way of Indians assuming
responsibility for their own lives and the training,
upbringing, of their children." Among these are the
notion that Indians are not quite human, and, therefore, not entitled to the land they used and occupied;
the notion that they have no law or government; and
the notion that children grow up without training or
discipline. Further, he cites "the notion, misconcep-
tion . . . that Indians are all hunters. They just roamed
over the land, had no title to it, and therefore the
incoming Europeans, since they were presumably all
farmers and husbandmen, made superior use of the
land and therefore were entitled to take it." The con-
nection of this last passage with that from the foreword quoted immediately before should be clear. It
is an undeniable fact of history that in coaxing a crop
from marginal lands, Indians have often succeeded

where whites have failed. In any case *Runner* represents a frontal assault on many negative stereotypes long prevalent in American culture, stereotypes which had as their common purpose to alienate Indians from their land.

Another stereotype that has proven to be tragic for Indian peoples through most of American history is the view of the Indian as a bloodthirsty savage. D'Arcy addresses this one in his foreword as well, in his reference to scientists digging into old village sites and finding no evidence of warfare:

> The myths and legends of the many tribes are not battle stories, but convey instead a feeling for the dignity of man and reverence for all of nature. Best of all evidence of the innate peace-seeking habits of the first Americans are the living Indian societies of today. Here one finds true concern for the well-being of each least member, respect for the elders, and devotion to the needs of the spirit.

Here McNickle demonstrates a continuity in Indian life and values from ancient times until the present, but his main concern, clearly, was the living Indian societies of his time and beyond. In telling of the first Americans he has pointed repeatedly to modern Indian societies as if to say that as long as Indians survive there is no reason for despair. They are the living embodiment of the peaceful ways of the ancient Americans, and they retain for present and future generations the greater gift we once "let lie . . . the gift of peace on earth."

Although the story in *Runner* takes place hundreds

of years before the New World was reintroduced to
the Old by Columbus, the Indian reality of the 1950s
is further represented in the novel, I believe. One
bit of evidence is the very way the story begins:

> This is the story of a town that refused to die. It is the
> story of the angry men who tried to destroy, and of the
> Indian boy called Salt, in the language of his people, who
> stood against them.
>   It was not an ordinary town. . . . One might travel close
> by and never know the town existed, unless one had been
> told about it.

The "town" referred to here may be more than the
village of the novel. It may refer to the Indian world
in general, a world silent and respectful, almost in-
visible by comparison to the white man's noisy society. The "angry men who tried to destroy" may not
be symbolic representations of white men, but they
would fit a description of the behavior of white col-
onists from Jamestown onward, as well as the pro-
ponents of the policies D'Arcy McNickle and other
Indian leaders were fighting in the years just pre-
ceding and just after publication of *Runner.*

The town in the story faces the end of a way of life.
The thirst for power on the part of one man creates
a schism in the village. Dark Dealer claims power
for his clan and turns the other clans out of the village.
The usurper wins over the rightful chief of the village,
at least at first. He says to the people who have been
chased out of the village that they have no choice but

to acknowledge his power and name him village chief, since they have no food, arms, or drinking water, having left everything inside the town. To this one of the clan chiefs replies: "We have stored up peace in our hearts, something you have forgotten. . . . Those who remember this and live accordingly will never be destroyed. . . . We will survive. . . ." (p. 144) Other words from D'Arcy's foreword can now be understood in an enhanced context: "Corn was, indeed, a great gift to the world; but a greater gift was one that the world let lie and never gathered up for its own. That was the gift of peace on earth." The clan chief's words explain why Dark Dealer would himself be the instrument of his own destruction. The Holy One himself maintained this, and Salt reflected on his wisdom: "Salt felt his blood warm at the fire of this old man's wisdom. Shame and outrage could come to a people, but they could still save themselves as long as their leaders remained firm." (p. 161) D'Arcy underscores here the importance of leadership, a subject to which he devoted much time and energy among modern Indian youth between 1956 and 1970.

We come now to the most important message in the book. The Holy One speaks: "Is it a new race of corn that is needed, then? I cannot say. Maybe what is needed is that our people should change. We are no longer the children we were when our songs, our dances, and our Mother Corn first came among us. We cannot live in fullness with these things as once we did. We try to reach beyond them." (p. 165) With

these words the Village Chief explains to Salt the
reasons for his journey. Utter destruction looms as a
possibility, and change provides the only possible so-
lution. Besides change, there is another factor, culture, the role of which we have inadequately
appreciated in determining Indian actions. Both
themes recur in D'Arcy's writing. Of change he notes
most explicitly: "Those who insist that Indians must
change their way of life if they are to survive are
really insisting that the change must be made at once.
They ignore or minimize the fact that Indians have
been changing their habits, their material culture,
and their outlook since the coming of the first white
man." As to the role of culture, D'Arcy observes suc-
cinctly: "If the Indian accepted some objects and customs from the white world, why did he not accept
them all?" Most whites have failed to understand that
the Indian used whatever he adopted "as a more
effective tool for carrying on the kind of life he knew."
As well, material acquisitions by themselves were
"not enough to overturn a whole system of experience."

From the interaction of these two factors, change
and culture, arises the problem of acculturation, or
culture change, which he dealt with in a different
way, first in *The Surrounded*, and later in *Wind from
an Enemy Sky*. In both novels tragedy is the obvious
consequence of a mistaken notion of acculturation,
one which assumes that is is entirely a one-way process. The problem D'Arcy presents us with in *Runner*

is the same, dealt with differently. Salt is the prototype of the modern Indian, for whom the only hope lies in change. He sets out on a journey, a process which can lead to knowledge and wisdom. Like Salt, the modern Indian must know the alien culture that surrounds him in order to get what he needs for his survival. In the first two novels we find the consequences of this process as it is erroneously understood by many. In *Runner* we find a statement of what it should be, a "creative process in which there is selection, rejection, and modification or adaptation of elements." Returning to Salt, "coming to the end of his journey, what was he to bring back with him? . . . He had come a long and difficult journey, and the thought that he might return home empty-handed filled him with anguish for his people." (p. 184) It may well have been that this same doubt gnawed at D'Arcy during the early 1950s, when all of his efforts on behalf of Indian people seemed to be coming to nothing, for surely he was on a journey similar to that of Salt.

Other elements in the book are significant, and reach beyond Salt's journey to the condition of the modern Indian. One is the respect shown by Salt for cultures different from his own. Salt never fails to pay respect to the shrines he finds on his way, and, thanks to this gesture, he goes on unmolested. D'Arcy also mentions the difficulties arising for Salt from the lack of a common language along his journey: "without knowledge of the language of the people he was to meet, he could never explain his mission, nor understand whatever they tried to tell him. Indeed, for lack of their speech, he might be slain as an enemy spy." (p. 184)

In the foreword, D'Arcy mentioned two gifts. *Runner* is the story of Indian maize. What about the other gift, the greater one in D'Arcy's words? Its decided omission heretofore makes our attention shift from one to the other. The new breed of corn Salt carries with him is soon endangered by drought. Such a frail gift cannot be expected to ensure the people's survival. If it is not corn, it is the other gift Salt brings back with him that is the one the people needed, the one he had been sent out to look for. This is the girl Quail. The way D'Arcy describes her makes this immediately clear:

> He turned to Quail and saw that her eyes were filled with the peace that lay before them. (pp. 219–20)

> Turning to her, Salt saw in her eyes the same look of peace. . . . (p. 224)

> Her eyes had never been so full of longing as they were then. Never had the vision of peace so filled them. (p. 227)

> "She will be one of us. We feel her strength entering into us." (p. 232)

Shortly after he and Quail return, Salt is named Village Chief by the dying Holy One, and he decides that his people must leave the town and move to a more fertile land. And it is Quail's presence that makes the separation of the people from their homeland less bitter. So *Runner* is not so much the story of Indian maize as the story of Quail, the story of peace on earth, of, even, that capacity for understanding that D'Arcy himself brought to his people after a journey which lasted fifty years.

In the story, Dark Dealer, who had been proud "beyond the reach of hunger," goes back to his people and asks to be forgiven on the same evening Salt returns. Salt expresses the wish that he be re-accepted and the people made whole again:

> "I think understanding is here among us," the Holy One spoke. . . .
> "It is not strange, I think, for our enemy to seek us out at this time. The power in this boy has pulled him—"
> The Holy One was looking directly at Salt, studying his face, his high, thin nose, his quiet eyes.
> "Power is here. The power to restore peace in a bad heart. The very power needed by our people. . . ."
> "If we ask ourselves how this power comes to this boy, I find that answer not strange either. Here is the girl, bearing some sign, perhaps of the sun, on her brow." (pp. 230–31)

Salt is about to reveal the real meaning of the slave mark, but he never does. In a way, he realizes that his people are right, and comes to share their feeling. At last he himself sees the power of the girl and understands that she is the gift so badly needed by his people:

> The words he would have uttered, explaining the slave mark, dissolved and were gone. The mark itself—the little

circle, with parallel lines running to the four directions—
glowed brightly as the girl stood before the firelight. And
the people spoke in wonder.

  Weariness fell away from Salt's limbs, and from his heart
as well. The disappointment which had been building so
steadily since he left Tula's house, tasting so bitter, was
fading like a dream at waking time. (p. 227)

In place of the disappointment, Salt realizes the
greatness of the gift he has brought to his people:
"Salt, looking across space, saw the slave girl vanish,
and beauty stand before him. His smile shone back
from her eyes." (p. 232)

  The form of *Runner in the Sun* is noteworthy. The
book is more explicitly connected with the oral tradition than are the author's other two novels. Everything about *Runner* suggests that it is a story about
Indians told in an Indian way; that is to say, it re-
sembles a story that is told more than one that is
written. Sentences are brief, coordination prevails
over subordination, and nouns are repeated rather
than represented by pronouns, to make the listener's
task easier. The narrator is obviously omniscient as
well, as in traditional tale-telling. The way D'Arcy
begins, with a grouping of short sentences telling the
subject matter of the story, is typical of such story-
telling. This is also true for the way the story finishes.
The direct narration of events ends before the real
ending of the book. A brief summary follows, with
one short sentence closing the book:

  So they left the Canyon of the White Rocks, which today
stands tenantless and soundless. They traveled southward,

down from the mountains, into the valley of the big fields. Land was set aside for them by those who were there first, and the new corn, when planted and watered abundantly, produced such harvests as had never been known. In their rejoicing the people performed a new ceremony, which they called Red Corn Dance. In time they built a great village of adobe walls, and dug canals to lead water from the river to their planted fields.

There they lived in peace and supported one another. (pp. 233–34) The rhythm is easily recognizable and similar to a tale from a well-thumbed copy of *Kutenai Tales* which D'Arcy had in his library:

When they got there, the youth had already killed all those who were not dead. He had killed them and taken their property.
Then the youth became a chief. Now I have told you how the old woman killed all the Kuyo' kwe.

Another tale from the same collection ends as follows: "Then the youth took the girl for his wife. Then the Kutenai increase from there. Now I have told you what happened long ago." Like the traditional Indian story teller, D'Arcy also uses his story to instruct. That is to say, he conveys a serious message, a meaning or truth on which listeners may reflect even while they are entertained. All of this demonstrates D'Arcy McNickle's fidelity to the oral tradition, where the higher aim is not to amuse but to instruct.

Alfonso Ortiz
University of New Mexico